WEREling

WEREling

STEVE FEASEY

FEIWEL AND FRIENDS
NEW YORK

A FEIWEL AND FRIENDS BOOK
An Imprint of Macmillan

WERELING. Copyright © 2009 by Steve Feasey. All rights reserved.
Printed in March 2010 in the United States of America by R. R. Donnelley & Sons
Company, Harrisonburg, Virginia. For information, address Feiwel and Friends,
175 Fifth Avenue, New York, N.Y. 10010.

A CIP catalogue record for this book is available from the British Library

ISBN: 978-0-312-59612-5

Originally published in the United Kingdom as *Changeling* by Macmillan
Children's Books, a division of Macmillan Publishers Limited

First published in the United States by Feiwel and Friends,
an imprint of Macmillan

Feiwel and Friends logo designed by Filomena Tuosto

First U.S. Edition: 2010

10 9 8 7 6 5 4 3 2 1

www.feiwelandfriends.com

For Zoe, who held my hand on the roller coaster and didn't insist that we ride the merry-go-round again.

And for my father, for all the books in the toilet. I miss you.

WEREling

1

Trey Laporte opened his eyes, wincing against the assault of the late-morning sunshine on his retinas. Sitting up in bed, he clutched his hands to his head as a mortar shell of pain exploded inside his brain. Bright stars lit up behind his eyelids, making him feel sick to his stomach. He sank back onto his pillow with a groan and stared up at the ceiling, which shifted and swirled slightly under his scrutiny. Saliva filled his mouth again and he concentrated hard on not vomiting, wishing that these feelings would go away.

He realized that he had no recollection of going to bed last night. He struggled to remember, small, tight lines creasing his forehead as he tried to piece together what could have happened to cause him to wake up feeling like this. But there was nothing.

After dinner he'd played Pro Evolution Soccer on the X-box with Wayne in the common room. Wayne was his usual inept self and Trey soon got bored of thrashing the pants off him. At nine o'clock he'd called it a night and gone back to his room to listen to his MP3 player. He'd walked into the room, locked it behind him, and then . . . nothing.

He couldn't remember a single thing from that moment onward. It was as if someone had hit a Delete button at the

1

precise moment he'd entered his room, and erased everything from that point until now.

He lifted himself up off the pillow again. A fresh wave of nausea rolled over him, causing a hiss to escape his lips. His mouth was so dry that his swollen tongue felt sticky against the roof of his palate. He needed a drink of water. He swung his legs over the edge of the bed, his eyes shut against both the sunlight and the fireworks that detonated inside his skull whenever he moved. He was naked. This fact bothered him because he never slept naked. He fished under his pillow and pulled out his pajama shorts. This was just too weird. Trey forced his eyes open and bent down to pull the shorts on when he saw his shoes. His favorite shoes. *What the hell . . . ?*

There was a sharp knock at the door.

Trey ignored the knock, and the pain, and the sickness that consumed every molecule of him. He'd saved for *weeks* to be able to afford those sneakers, and now they were lying on the floor ripped apart as though someone had taken a large carving knife and slashed at them in some frenzied attack. He leaned forward to get a closer look at the mess and gasped as the rush of blood to his head caused a balloon of pain to burst behind his eyes.

"My shoes! What the . . . ?" His voice cracked as he tried to speak, and his throat felt painfully raw. The pain pulsated through his esophagus in waves, and he instinctively reached up a hand to touch the flesh around his throat. He swallowed, wincing at the pain that even this simple act caused. Standing up, he desperately looked around for something to drink, and saw properly for the first time the chaos that had become his bedroom. He turned in a slow circle, his mouth hanging open in utter disbelief as he took in the destruction and disorder that was all around him.

He shivered and became aware of the cold for the first time. Looking over his shoulder, he stared at the window, which was hanging at an impossible angle from the buckled metal casing. Large gouges could be seen on the frame where the white plastic had been scored away, revealing the shiny metal underneath. The window itself was intact but appeared to have been torn away from the top hinge so that it hung outward at a drunken incline. His eyes shifted to the wall to the side of the opening, where great rents had been made in the plaster, as if someone had taken a garden fork and raked it along the surface.

How could he have slept through this? How could anyone have slept through this?

The entire room had been wrecked. His possessions—he had so few good things that he kept them neatly arranged and cared for—were scattered around the place, many broken and destroyed. His heart was slamming into his chest and he felt a sudden urge to scream out in anger. He wanted to cry. He wanted to kill someone. He wanted to find whoever had done this and—

The knock on the door was repeated, louder this time, and he turned to look in its direction. His eyes fell on the

3

key that was still in the lock on the inside. He walked over and twisted the door handle, expecting to feel the door give and open. He stepped back when it refused to budge and stared suspiciously at the white glossy surface. Reaching forward again, he took the key between his thumb and finger and slowly turned it clockwise, the lines on his forehead deepening at the sound of the bolt sliding free from the plate in the door and receding back into the body of the mechanism. He let the door open an inch or two. Turning his head, he looked over again at the window, noting that the key was still in that lock too. His heart shifted up a gear, and he looked around the room again in dismay, unable to even begin to try to piece together what had happened here. A desire to throw up came over him.

The damage to the window looked as if it had been done from the inside . . . and yet he had been in the room asleep. Surely he would have woken up at the sound of all this carnage going on around him.

Trey slowly turned around and went back over to the bed. He picked up his ruined sneakers, ignoring the daggers of pain that stabbed at his brain, and sat on the mattress, staring down at the ripped leather-and-rubber jumble that had so recently been his prized possession—the best pair of shoes he had ever owned.

They look like some kind of dissected animals, he thought, and he was reminded of the frogs that they had been made to cut apart in a biology class, their tough outer skins sliced open and then peeled back to reveal the gory

4

interiors. The laces that he'd spent so long getting just right—he'd rethreaded them three times so that the bars would not be twisted—were now a ruptured, shredded mess.

"Trey?" Colin Wallington's voice came into the room. "Are you all right, Trey?"

The door was pushed open a little farther and Trey heard the gasp.

"Oh my God. What have you done?"

Colin Wallington stepped into the room. He was a tall, skinny man with black slicked-back hair and greedy eyes that never stayed still. These, coupled with a thin, hooked nose, gave him an unkind, birdlike appearance that had earned him the nickname of Vulture from the children in his care. He walked into the center of the room, gawking about him in disbelief and shaking his head. He turned to stare at Trey with a look of rage.

"What have you done here?"

"Are you mad?" Trey croaked. "I didn't do this. Why would I do this to *my* room and *my* stuff? Look at these shoes!" He held them up for a second before realizing that he was still completely naked. He pulled the quilt over his lower half and reached for his pajamas again, pulling them on over his legs beneath the covers.

Trey noticed that Colin was shaking as he stood, rooted to the spot, some galvanizing current running through his entire body anchoring him in position. He was clenching and unclenching his left hand as he looked at the teenager.

5

Trey had never seen the head care worker of Apple Grove Care Home so angry in the three years that he had been there. Colin was a hurtful, spiteful man, who seemed to derive some sick kind of pleasure from belittling the children in his care, but as far as Trey was aware, he had never physically harmed anyone in his charge. Instead he was an insidious bully who relied upon harsh and unkind words to hurt the kids he didn't like. Trey had never seen him as worked up as he was now, and was fearful that the man might actually be on the verge of hitting him.

"Do you have any idea how much trouble and extra work you have caused me with this little stunt?" Colin asked through clenched teeth. A tic had started up above his left eyebrow, causing it to twitch repetitively. "I'll have to file a report, get someone in to fix that window, and—"

He stopped and sniffed, his face contorting into a gargoyle-like caricature of disgust, the tic still merrily dancing to some unheard tune over his eye.

"What in God's name is that stench?"

He bent and picked up the tattered sweatshirt at his feet. Smelling it and deciding that this was not the source of the reek that filled the room, he dropped it and eyed Trey suspiciously. "What have you been *doing* in here, you disgusting little turd?"

Trey could smell it now. It was an oily, metallic smell that reminded him of rotting leaves and freshly turned earth. But there was something else lying within the odor that was not so easy to identify. A brownish-orange smell, which, although strangely familiar to him, just eluded his attempts to identify it.

He stopped. Brownish-orange smell? What on earth was he thinking? You don't see odors, you just . . . smell them.

But that was exactly how he envisioned this smell that permeated through the room, as a rich, gravy-like color, with slowly pulsating globes of orange moving around within it—but even *color* wasn't the right word to describe the feeling he was trying to pin down. It was more like a *memory* of a sensation, some innate sense that he had either lost or never used before—like being blind from birth and trying to describe how you *see* the sky in your mind's eye.

Frowning, he shook his head, trying to rattle loose these strange thoughts and clear them out.

"Are you listening to me?" Colin said, pointing a shaking finger at him. "This," he said, staring around him again, "is too much. Even for you. I thought that we were beyond the anger issues that you brought with you when you came here three years ago. But clearly you need to be reminded of how to behave like a human being again. I'm going to refer you for a little *vacation* in the APU. Remember your last stay there? I'm sure you'll feel right back at home once you're on a ward surrounded by a whole gang of other psychopaths. Pack your stuff—you'll be leaving for the Tank today."

The Tank was a referral center for the Adolescent Psychiatric Unit where Apple Grove sent kids that had gone off the rails. Self-harmers, kids who were at risk of suicide, violent and abusive children were all sent to the APU. The unit itself wasn't so bad, but before you got there you had to go to the Tank, where the approach to keeping you quiet was to fill you so full of drugs that you became one of the living dead. Trey had been sent there five months after his arrival at the home when his refusal to communicate with anyone, coupled with beating up a boy named Matthew Cotter, was deemed serious enough to warrant a visit. What the care home failed to realize was that Matthew Cotter had been the cause of Trey's refusal to talk and that he had been flushing Trey's head down the toilet every day for all of those five months until the day Trey had snapped and fought back, putting the bully in the hospital with a broken nose.

"Colin, I've already told you," Trey said, with a wince. Just talking was extremely painful. "I didn't do any of this. Why on earth would I? You can't send me to the Tank for something I didn't do. Just listen to me. I don't know how—"

"I don't want to hear it, Mr. Laporte. Now pack your stuff."

"But."

"Pack your stuff . . . NOW."

"*Whatever.*" Trey glared at the care worker with utter contempt. "I've only had those shoes a week!" He kicked out at one of the sneakers, lost his footing and fell back on the mattress again, where he sat scowling down at the floor. He was feeling progressively more unwell; he ached all over as if in the early stages of a virus.

"I think I must have been drugged," he said meekly, shaking his head at how lame that sounded. "Someone must have slipped something in my food or drink and then managed to break in here after me and do all this."

"Oh yes, that's right. Maybe Belinda or one of the other carers dropped some Rohypnol into your tea while you weren't looking so that they could come in here and smash the place up. Then, unseen, they carried you back in here and locked the door from the inside. Perhaps they're hiding under the bed right now? Come on, Trey, credit me with some intelligence, will you?"

A deep sea of resentment rose up within Trey at the injustice of the whole situation. He clenched his fists and tried to control the anger that was building up inside him. He was the one who had been wronged here. It was *his* room and possessions that had been violated and destroyed, and here he was being accused of that very act. The brown-orange smell seemed to be getting stronger, and he felt the need to bellow his fury at the world. He was vaguely aware that the smell seemed to be coming from him, and it was coupled with an uncomfortable itching feeling in the base of his spine, which quickly grew into an unbearable ache.

There was another knock at the door.

"Not now," shouted Colin. "We're not finished in here yet! I won't tell you again, Trey. Pack your stuff."

Trey doubled over in pain as the spasms increased in intensity. His whole body felt incredibly hot and the itching ache had spread so that all the skin on his body had

9

become a source of exquisite agony. His stomach rolled and he gagged. "Colin, I'm telling you, I . . . ungh—"

"Oh, how convenient," the care worker sneered. "We get to the point where only the truth will fit the facts and you get ill! What? Do you think this little act will save you from being sent to the Tank? Well, think again."

The soft, hesitant knock on the door was repeated, and when it opened, Wendy Travers's head appeared around the doorjamb. Wendy was a young woman with a kind face and a laugh that erupted from her whenever she was nervous or embarrassed—which was often. She was by far the nicest care worker in the home, and Trey admired how she always went the extra mile for the younger children, especially those who were new to the care environment.

"Wendy, love, not right now, please. Young Trey and I are trying to get to the bottom of what has happened here and he appears to have rather fortuitously come over all peculiar."

Wendy quickly took in the mess of the small room before turning her attention back to her boss. "I'm sorry. It's just that it is rather important, Colin."

"So is this. So if you would be so kind as to leave us alone, I'll deal with whatever it is when I get finished in here."

Wendy chewed her bottom lip as she considered this, the small frown on her forehead deepening. Eventually she took a breath and announced, "Trey's got a visitor. There's a gentleman in reception who says that he'd like to see him.

He says he's his uncle." Wendy smiled up at Colin apologetically before looking over in Trey's direction. The look on her face was difficult to decipher, but Trey thought that she looked deeply uncomfortable and more than a little scared.

Trey slowly straightened up. The waves of pain that had so quickly escalated started to recede as he took in this announcement. He looked for a clue in Wendy's face to see if she was playing some kind of trick on him—although it would have been completely out of character for her to do such a thing—but her features merely mirrored his own puzzled expression.

Trey had no family. He was an orphan whose only living relative, his grandmother, had died three years earlier. After her death, the authorities had tried to find any extended family to ascertain if there might be someone willing to take him in, but none could be found, so he'd ended up in care.

Trey never had visitors, and he made a point of not being around on visiting days so as not to have to witness the buzz of excitement that took over the care home when the children knew that someone from the outside world was coming to see them. Today wasn't even a visiting day.

"What should I do?" Wendy asked. "He was very insistent and said that it was a matter of the utmost urgency."

Colin paused for a second and looked over at the fourteen-year-old boy in his charge. "Ask him to wait in the contact room, please, Wendy, and tell him that I shall be in shortly."

He turned back to Trey as the door clicked shut, an unpleasant sneer playing across his thin, mean lips. "Well, well. What do you know? Some long-lost relative riding in on his white horse to rescue little orphan Annie. You'd better put some proper clothes on, if you can find any in this chaos. Wait in here until I find out what this is all about." He gestured with his thumb toward the window. "And don't think for one second that you have heard the last about this little caper," he said.

He turned and left the room, kicking the ruined trainers out of his way as he left.

2

Trey stood up and moved over to the door as soon as Colin had shut it. He pressed his ear to the surface, listening intently for any noise on the other side. Colin called out to somebody and was answered by the sound of approaching footsteps. Strain as he might, Trey couldn't make out the details of what was being said in the corridor outside his room. It didn't matter; Trey knew that Colin would be asking whoever it was to keep an eye on his room to ensure that he stayed inside and didn't come out. He pulled some clothes out of his dirty washing basket and threw them on as quickly as he could. He stalked around the room, trying to come up with a plan. Leaving by the door was out of the question, and all the windows in the home were security windows that would open only a fraction of the way. Trey stopped and turned to look at his window again. The security of this window had been well and truly breached. If he climbed out of the ruined mess, he could make his way around the back of the building and re-enter at the staff entrance. There was a numerical keypad to gain entry, but all the kids in the home knew the combination. He just had to hope that it had not been changed in the last week or so.

He clambered out of the window, being careful not to

cut himself on the jagged edges of the metal frame, and dropped down into a rosebush that happily did the job instead. Ignoring the pain in his hands and legs, he looked around him. He didn't expect anyone to be on the grounds, but it wouldn't do to be caught sneaking around like this. Stooping over and keeping low so that he would not be spotted, he ran along the back of the building. At the front, he used the parked cars as cover, darting between each one until he was standing outside the staff door. He paused to get his breath back for a moment and then entered the four-digit code into the keypad; the buzzing sound that resulted indicated that the code was still good and that the door was now open. He pushed his way inside and crept forward, scanning the corridor for any signs of staff members.

Trey stood outside the rear entrance to the contact room. He glanced up the hall to ensure that nobody was coming and placed his ear against the cold, glossed surface of the door, trying to hear what was going on inside. The contact room was L-shaped, with doors at either end so that families could be brought in from one end and children from the other. This way, if the meeting went very badly, the two parties could be ushered away in separate directions with the minimum amount of fuss. Trey hoped that Colin and the visitor claiming to be his uncle were at the other end, and the lack of any voices through the door he was listening at seemed to confirm this. He pushed very gently against the metal hand plate, holding his breath and grimacing up at the hydraulic damper at the top of the door that hissed as he pushed against it. Slipping through the small gap that he had created, he entered the room as swiftly and silently as he could, relieved this time when the damper did its job properly and gently brought the door to a close without a sound. He'd guessed correctly—this end of the room was empty—and he silently made his way to the corner of the L so that he could listen in on what was being said.

Colin was in the middle of his usual welcome speech in which he recounted facts about the number of children that the home had helped and how proud he was to be part of such a worthwhile establishment.

Unable to resist a peek at the mysterious visitor, Trey dropped down onto his haunches so that he could peer around the corner with one eye, certain that he would not be spotted if he kept as low as possible.

The visitor stood with his back to Trey and appeared to be admiring the view of the garden through the French windows off to his left while Colin prattled on. Wendy was also in the room, leaning against the wall just inside the far entrance and trying to distance herself from the scene as much as possible. She played with a loose strand of her hair, curling and uncurling it around her index finger between casting furtive looks at the stranger.

". . . for the delay, but we've had a minor crisis that needed to be sorted out and weren't expecting any visitors. Mr. . . . ?" said Colin, extending his hand in greeting and walking toward the man in the center of the room.

Trey noted the way that the care worker's fingers wilted

15

as they extended from his outstretched palm and instinctively knew that Colin Wallington's handshake would be a limp, impotent affair.

The man in the gray suit turned around to face Colin for the first time. He was a little over six feet tall and was athletically built beneath his well-cut suit. His head was perfectly shaven; the pale dome reflecting back the light from the tungsten bulbs set into the ceiling above. A black and gray neat goatee framed his wide mouth. Despite the low level of lighting in the room, he wore black sunglasses that obscured his eyes and reflected back a smoky image of his surroundings as well as the man standing in front of him. Trey guessed that he would be considered handsome by women, and a quick glance over at Wendy's expression as she stared at the tall visitor seemed to confirm this suspicion.

In his right hand, the man held a horn-handled umbrella, but he made no attempt to transfer this to his left in order to take up the proffered handshake.

"Please, call me Lucien," the man said.

He turned his head slightly and appeared to glance toward the corner behind which Trey was hiding. The briefest hint of a smile played across his features. He seemed to be looking directly at Trey, although it was impossible to be certain with those mirrored lenses covering his eyes. Trey withdrew his head and held his breath.

There was a long pause as if the stranger was considering how to continue. Eventually he said in a loud voice,

16

"You know, Trey, it really must be very uncomfortable being hunched down like that for any period of time. I think that it would be better for everyone if you just came out and joined us. It really is rather rude to spy on people."

Trey shook his head in disbelief at what had just happened. The man had had his back turned to him when Trey had snuck in, and the boy was certain that he could not have caught sight of him in the mirrored reflection of the room thrown back by the windows to his left. He weighed up his options: He could leg it back to his room and pretend that he didn't know what Colin was on about if he was asked, or he could face up to being caught and find out who this stranger was.

The frown on Colin Wallington's face fell away into an angry scowl as Trey sheepishly stepped out from around the corner. The care worker opened his mouth to say something, but then thought better of it. He gestured for the boy to come toward them before turning back to their visitor with a sickly smile, but the man calling himself Lucien was no longer looking in his direction. Instead, the mirrored lenses were now firmly fixed on Trey.

"As I was saying . . . Lucien," Colin continued, "we really were not expecting you. This is not one of our designated visiting dates, and while we can, under special circumstances, arrange for visitation rights outside of these times, we do have a strict policy that requires a twenty-four-hour notice of intent—so that we can prepare properly. In addition, as we have no way of knowing that you are who

17

you say you are, we would need to run the appropriate checks before visitation rights could be granted. I'm sure that you will understand that as the head care worker at the home, I would be neglecting my duties if I did not adhere to these rules."

Trey watched as Colin folded his arms and plastered a "What-can-you-do?" smile on his face.

A silence filled the room which would have been complete were it not for the low hum of the extractor fan set in one of the windows.

The stranger stood, unmoving, for what seemed like an age, and Trey could feel his eyes drilling into him from behind the dark glasses.

Eventually, the man claiming to be Trey's uncle slowly reached into his suit jacket and retrieved a folded sheet of paper and a passport from the internal breast pocket. He held these out for Colin to examine.

"I have brought a birth certificate and a passport to prove my identity, Mr. Wallington. And as I explained to your charming assistant, Miss Travers, I would not have come and imposed myself on you in this manner if it were not of the utmost necessity to do so." He slowly reached up and removed the glasses from his eyes, folding them and placing them in the top pocket of his suit.

When he turned to look back at Trey, the boy felt an involuntary shudder run through him to the core.

The man's eyes were, well, *freakish*.

The irises were a light honey-brown interspersed with

tiny flecks of ocher that became more dominant toward the center of the eye, until eventually the lighter spots merged into a central ring around the black of the pupil. Trey was torn between the desire to step closer and look into these fascinating pools of color and the more powerful wish to turn away and escape their insidious glare. Much to his relief, the tall man switched his attention to Colin.

He stepped forward, handing over the documents. Trey, unable to take his eyes off him, was amused when, out of the corner of his eye, he noticed Colin take an immediate step backward in response.

"Please, feel free to contact whichever authorities you consider necessary," said the tall stranger, pressing the ID papers into the care worker's hands. "I fully understand the difficult position that I have put you and your establishment in by simply turning up unannounced in this way, but I merely wish to have ten minutes with my nephew here. I have some very important information that I must share with him."

"Believe me, Mr. . . ." Colin's nervous fingers fumbled open the back page of the passport to reveal the stranger's details. "Mr. Laporte, I truly do wish that it were as simple as that. But there are protocols in place that . . ."

Trey subconsciously filtered out the rest of Colin's speech as his mind began to try to make sense of what he had just heard. It surprised him to hear his surname associated with this man standing in front of him, because whoever this mysterious stranger was, there was one thing that Trey was absolutely convinced of: This man was not his uncle.

". . . rules are there for the safety of the children in our care. I'm sorry, but I really have to insist on you leaving now." Colin finished and held out the papers at arm's length to return them to their owner.

The man calling himself Lucien Laporte calmly accepted the papers and returned them to his jacket pocket. He sighed and drew himself up to his full height, fixing his gaze on an invisible spot somewhere above the care worker's head. A hard, humorless smile crept slowly across his lips as he took this in and considered how to proceed. Finally he turned to look at Wendy, the smile genuine now and displaying teeth that were perfectly white and set in a face that was at once both alarming and handsome.

"Miss Travers—Wendy, isn't it?" he said in a calm voice. "I wonder if you would be so kind as to get me a glass of water. It would seem that my visit has been fruitless, and I would appreciate a drink before I take the long journey back home."

Wendy flushed red and self-consciously reached down to straighten the hem of her skirt, and for one horrible moment, Trey thought that she was going to curtsy. "That won't be any trouble, Mr. Laporte. I'll just pop down to the kitchen." She stopped at the door to look back worriedly in Colin's direction before leaving.

The door slowly closed with a soft thud. A fly had got

into the room and was noisily attacking the glass of the windowpane as it sought a means of escape. Its buzz-tap, buzz-tap attempts at freedom punctuated the silence that now filled the room.

"Mr. Wallington," the stranger said, "I am not an unreasonable man, and I have explained to you that I fully understand the position that I am putting you in, but I have just driven for two hours to get here and all I request of you today is ten minutes alone with Trey. After that I will leave and you can make whatever checks you must in order to establish that I really am who I say I am." His eyes dropped momentarily and he examined the handle of the umbrella in his hand. When he looked up again, he spoke in a low, conspiratorial tone.

"I know that you have a great responsibility to the children in your charge, Mr. Wallington. And I give you my word of honor that I would never do anything to undermine the trust that has been placed in you to carry out those responsibilities. I also know that you have the authority to grant me my request and I appeal to your better nature to allow me this audience with my nephew."

"I'm afraid that I simply cannot allow—"

Lucien cut him off with a gesture of his hand, and Trey saw a sudden intensity in his eyes that made them blaze in their sockets, like a fire suddenly flaring up upon finding a source of fuel to feed upon.

There was a perfect *stop* then. A complete and absolute cessation of *everything*. Trey involuntarily held his breath at the strangeness of the moment. An utter silence pressed in upon the room. The whirr of the ventilation fan ceased, and when Trey glanced over to see the cause of its sudden silence, he spotted the little fly lying dead upon its back on the windowsill. Trey's mouth had gone completely dry, and he thought that the sound of his ragged breathing must have been audible to everyone in that terrible silence. He looked over at the tiny dead creature again and felt peculiarly unhinged by the sight of it lying there. He swallowed, hoping that he might be able to raise some saliva by doing so. Turning his attention back to the two men, he noted the look of abject fear on Colin's upturned face as Lucien's voice sliced through this strange void.

"I am an immensely rich and powerful man, Mr. Wallington, and while I choose not to wield these influences like some bludgeoning weapon, I think that you should know that I have considerable sway with a broad range of those *authorities* that you alluded to earlier. I believe that they may be extremely interested to know some of the more *intimate details* about the head care worker of this establishment." He leaned forward so that his nose was almost touching the hooked beak of the smaller man, his eyes steely as he continued.

"I am sure, for instance, that they would be extremely interested to find out how you have been embezzling funds from the care home's coffers into a bank account set up in your wife's name. They might also be disturbed to find out how young James Longton really broke his arm on the field trip to Cheshire last year."

Colin Wallington stared back at his accuser, a look of utter horror on his face.

"What the . . . ?" he stammered.

"Perhaps of most interest to them would be—"

"Uncle Lucien, that's enough," Trey said. "I think that you've made your point." Trey looked over at the care worker, who seemed to be unraveling before his very eyes.

There was a long pause. The nod that eventually came from the tall stranger was barely perceptible, but it seemed to Trey that the light that was ignited behind those oddly colored eyes had already dimmed, leaving them none the less fascinating, but reassuringly less frightening than they had been only moments before.

Trey had long dreamed of seeing his nemesis reduced to a state of crippling wretchedness, but witnessing Colin cringe and flinch at each of these revelations, the look of fear and revulsion in his eyes, had been too much even for him. He felt his own face burn in embarrassment for the man and could hardly bear to look at him.

Behind him, he heard the fan click back into operation, followed by the familiar buzz-tap of the little insect throwing itself once more against the window. He could almost sense the molecules in the air resume their random collisions with each other as the Pause button that had been activated upon the universe was switched back to Play. He flicked his eyes toward the window, and the sight of the fly bouncing off the glass again caused icy fingers to trace their way down his spine. The creature had been dead. He held his breath and listened to the minuscule sound of its headlong charge into the glass. It wasn't possible. What had just happened was not possible. He shifted his gaze back to the man called Lucien. Whatever he had just witnessed had been something to do with the visitor—he was certain of that.

Colin Wallington was covered in a film of sweat. He appeared to Trey to have become visibly smaller than he had been before this confrontation. The usual overconfident sneer was nowhere to be seen.

"Who are you?" Colin asked.

"I've already told you my name, Mr. Wallington. Now perhaps you would be so kind as to leave the two of us alone for a short while. Young Trey and I have important matters to discuss."

The care worker hesitated before replying in a small voice, "As you say, Mr. Laporte, I do indeed have the power to grant this meeting. However, I cannot force the boy to speak to you against his wishes, so the final decision must be Trey's."

He turned to Trey, a look of desperation on his face. Trey couldn't decipher whether the man was appealing to his better nature by urging him to agree, or simply willing him to refuse the meeting to help him salvage some small victory from the whole affair. In any case, he didn't much care what Colin hoped he would do; he had worries enough of his own at this precise moment.

"Well, Trey? Are you happy with me leaving you in the company of this man, your . . . uncle?"

Trey looked from Colin to the tall, bald-headed stranger. He was certain that if the man meant to do him any harm, he could quite easily have done so, regardless of how many of the care staff might or might not have been present. Because of this, and because there was something about this unnerving visitor's manner that suggested that it might truly be in his interest to speak to him, he nodded his assent.

"Sure," he said. "Why not?"

"Excellent," Lucien said, at once reverting to the clipped, business-like tone and manner that he had assumed during the initial introductions. "Thank you, Mr. Wallington. I appreciate your help in this matter. Now, if you would be so kind, my nephew and I have a lot of catching up to do. Oh, and could I possibly ask you to change my order with the delightful Wendy? I would much rather have a nice cup of tea, if that is not *too* much trouble."

Colin pushed with irritation at the displaced strands of his hair that had escaped their slicked-down confines and went to leave the room. Stopping at the door, he turned, smiling uneasily. "If you need any help, Trey, Wendy and I will be just along the corridor in the kitchen fixing our *guest's* tea."

Lucien waited until the door had completely shut before

turning to face Trey: His smile was open and genuine. Trey had the same feeling of being completely disarmed that he was sure Wendy had felt when that look had been directed at her. He shook the well-manicured hand that was being offered to him.

"Well, young Trey Laporte, where should we begin?"

3

"How about you begin by telling me who you really are, *Uncle Lucien*?"

That smile came back to his visitor's face, and he motioned for them to sit down on the sofa.

"My name really is Lucien, but my surname—as you have already deduced—is not Laporte: It is Charron."

"But the passport and the birth certificate . . ."

Lucien waved a hand in the air. "These things can be bought for the right price if you know the right people, Trey. It was my hope that by having those things with me that we would have been able to avoid that disagreeable scene you were just forced to witness." He shifted in his seat so that he completely faced Trey. "My apologies for that—it must have been rather unpleasant for you."

"Those things that you said about Mr. Wallington. Were they true?"

"I never tell lies, Trey. I may choose not to answer all questions that might be put to me, and I might even substitute one truth for another, but I don't lie. So, yes, all of those things were true."

"You lied about your name."

The stranger inclined his head as if considering this. "No.

27

I told him that my name is Lucien. The papers that I handed to him had my photograph next to the name Lucien Laporte, but I never told him that that was what I was called."

Trey considered this, but was uncomfortable about the ambiguity of Lucien's argument.

"What happened in the room just then?" Trey blurted out.

"How do you mean?"

"You held up your hand and everything . . . everything stopped. That fly over there—" Trey nodded in the direction of the window. "It died and then it . . ."

The quizzical look on Lucien's face caused Trey to flush a deep shade of red. "Sorry, I'm not making any sense. It's just that I thought . . . I thought that . . ."

"You thought that fly over there was dead?"

Trey nodded his head. Everything that had happened to him already this morning had clearly had more of an impact than he had imagined. He was making a fool of himself, babbling on about dead flies to this strange man.

"How could you possibly have found out all those dreadful things about Colin?" he eventually asked.

Lucien frowned, considering how to answer this question. "All men have secrets that they hide away. Some men try to keep them hidden in the deepest, darkest recesses of their being. But these secrets lie in wait, biding their time until they are eventually uncovered, and then they emerge, their fangs bared, ready to pierce the hearts of those who have kept them imprisoned for so long."

"You haven't answered my question."

"It is not an easy question to answer, Trey. Not in the short time that we have available to us now. Let us just say that I have a gift for peering into the more clandestine areas of a man's makeup. Like looking through a window to see what happens in the locked room beyond."

Trey turned to look at the man sitting next to him. Something about the way that he'd referred to locked rooms had been deliberately employed to strike a chord with him. His intense stare was mirrored unflinchingly until, with a slight raise of his eyebrow, Lucien broke the silence.

"Is everything OK, Trey?" His eyes softened again and that boyish smile played across his face.

"It was you, wasn't it? You were responsible for trashing my room and destroying my possessions last night, weren't you?" Trey stood up, looking down at the man on the sofa. Lucien peered down at the material of his suit and picked at an invisible fleck of something on his trousers.

"Your Mr. Wallington may have been wrong about a number of things, Trey, but I am afraid he was completely correct in his assumption as to who was responsible for the events that took place in your bedroom yesterday."

"You're lying," Trey insisted, his voice wavering. "If you had nothing to do with it, how come you know anything about it?"

"I've told you already, I don't lie. You yourself have just told me what occurred in your room last night. Sit down, Trey, please." He nodded back at the seat next to him.

Trey closed his eyes and blew out his cheeks. His head was whirling with everything that had already gone on, and he was struggling to keep himself together. He wanted nothing more than to return to his bed, crawl under the covers, and wait until everything simply went away.

Lucien looked at him and smiled sadly. "I imagine that you are feeling very frightened and confused right now. And that you are looking for some answers to the things that have happened to you since, and during, last night."

"And you can provide those answers?"

"A great many of them, yes. You see, I know—"

Trey exploded, "Don't say you know how I feel! Right now you have no idea how I feel. You don't know anything about me."

Lucien looked up at Trey with a look of genuine concern. He glanced at the clock on the wall above the door and, making his mind up about something, nodded at the boy.

"You're right, of course," he said. He paused before continuing cautiously. "However, not all of what you have said is correct. You and I have indeed met before, but you were a very small child and would not remember the encounter." He placed his hands upon his knees and leaned forward slightly. When he spoke again, his voice was calm and clear, but filled with a passion that had hitherto been absent.

"You see, I knew your mother and father. Indeed, we were great friends—your father and I worked together for a

30

long time. It was important, perilous work of the kind that forges eternal bonds between people. When you were born, your father rightly decided that he could no longer continue with our work and we drifted apart for a while. I visited your parents when you were three years old and I had never seen the two of them so happy. My fear was that my presence would inevitably blight that happiness, and as I have said, I was too fond of your father to allow that to happen. So I vowed that I would not interfere with their lives again. I kept that promise as best I could, asking for your father's help only in cases of extreme need."

He paused, considering how to continue. "For the happiness they knew during those early years of your life, I am forever grateful that I maintained my distance, but I earnestly believe that had I not put such a distance between us, they might still be alive today. I feel somewhat responsible for their deaths, and even more responsible for your safety. That is what I am doing here today, Trey. Please believe me when I say that I have kept a constant vigil over your welfare, and that I would not have hesitated to become involved in your life earlier had there been any signs that you were in imminent danger."

He stood up now and placed his hand on the boy's shoulder. "But what happened last night has changed everything. You are now in the danger that I have just alluded to, and I am here to keep you from harm."

"I don't understand any of this," Trey said.

"I know. But we are running out of time. Our odious little

friend Mr. Wallington will be back very shortly, and then there will be no way for me to protect you and to tell you all of the things that you really have to know about yourself and the dangers that you are in.

"I want you to have something." Lucien reached into his trouser pocket and opened his hand, revealing a silver chain and pendant. Picking up the chain, he held it up so that Trey could see it properly. The chain was very long, so that, as tall as he was, Lucien still had to hold the end high above the boy's head in order that he could see the ornament hanging from the bottom links.

The pendant was actually a small silver clenched fist. Trey reached up to hold it so that he could examine it more closely.

"What is this?" he asked.

"It was your father's. He would have wanted you to have it. And to wear it. Please, allow me." Lucien leaned forward and placed the chain around Trey's neck. He stood back, smiling at what he saw.

Trey looked down at the chain hanging down the outside of his T-shirt. He'd never worn any jewelry, and it felt heavy and odd to him. The pendant seemed to be hanging too far down, resting just above his navel.

"Why is it so long?" he asked, toying with the silver amulet.

"Because it needs to be. You don't want it coming off . . . *ever*." Lucien's gaze was unnerving, as if trying to drill home the significance of this last statement.

32

"Now, I suggest that you tuck it into your T-shirt and try to forget about it for a while." He reached for his umbrella and glanced at the expensive-looking watch hidden behind the folds of his cuff-linked sleeves.

"Trey, I must ask you something that is the key to what will happen next. It is a simple question, but, like all questions of that type, requires a deep and clearly considered response. Know that your answer will have a profound effect on your life from now on and that dire consequences may result if you make the wrong choice." He stopped to look over Trey's shoulder at the door and seemed to be listening for something.

"What are you—"

"Shh," Lucien cut him off with a raised hand, and then, seemingly happy with whatever it was that he had discovered, switched his attention back to the teenager.

Placing both hands on Trey's shoulders, he looked down at the boy and spoke to him with the same intensity that he had when he had spoken of Trey's parents.

"Trey, we have no time left. As of last night, your life has changed forever. Things will happen to you that you cannot hope to deal with on your own, and because of these things you are in terrible danger." He stared into Trey's eyes. "I need you to tell me something. Do you believe that you can trust me and that I am here to help you?" he said.

Trey looked up at the stranger's face, hoping to find some clue that could help him make sense of what was going on. He shook his head. He didn't believe that the man had any intention of hurting him, and yet . . .

Sensing his apprehension, Lucien bent forward until his face was on the same level as Trey's. "Your father loved you very much, Trey. Whether he had some inkling of what was to become of him, I don't know, but shortly before he died he asked me to promise to do something if anything should happen to him." Lucien smiled sadly. "Do you remember the nickname that your father had for you when you were a child, Trey?"

"Yes. He used to call me Little Loop. My grandmother told me."

A flicker of confusion crossed Lucien's face but was instantly replaced by a broad smile as he took in what Trey had said.

"Little Loop. That's very good. It's lost a little in translation, though."

"Lucien, what has all this got to do with—"

"'*Protège mon petit loup*'—those were the words that your father said to me that evening. He told me that if anything should happen to him, I was to protect his . . . little loop. And I agreed that I would. That is why I am here tonight, Trey: to keep a promise that I made to your father that night all those years ago. So I have to ask you again, do you trust me? Are you willing to place your life in my hands, knowing that I will allow no harm to come to you while there is an ounce of strength left in my body?"

Trey's hand involuntarily felt for the small silver

34

fist beneath his T-shirt and his fingers closed around the hard, solid shape. He looked at this stranger and considered everything that he had told him so far that day. He did believe that Lucien was there to help him in some way, and there was no doubting that the man seemed to sincerely believe that Trey was in some terrible danger. But it seemed an impossible question to answer. He needed more time. Everything was happening too quickly.

Lucien gently squeezed the top of his shoulders, urging a response from him. "Please, Trey. We do not have much time left. There are . . . forces at work that spell great danger for you. Even as we speak, they are moving against us. Will you trust me and let me help you as I promised?"

"Yes, Lucien. I do believe that you are here to help me and I do trust you. But—"

"Good man . . . and thank you." He grabbed the boy's arm and, gently lifting him to his feet, propelled him toward the door. "Come on, we are leaving this place. We need to go now, or the moment will be lost and I fear that another, *much* more unpleasant scene will ensue."

They left the room, turning to their right, and hurried down the corridor away from the direction of the kitchen.

Trey's mind was a mess of tumbling thoughts and emotions. One second he'd been sitting listening to Lucien telling him things about his parents, the next he was being physically propelled through the corridors of the care home as if his very life depended on it.

"The front door is the other way," Trey said, glancing over his shoulder.

"Indeed it is, but the emergency exit is this way." Lucien was walking extremely quickly, and his long legs made it impossible for Trey to keep up without jogging along beside him. He was still being steered by Lucien's firm grip on his upper arm, and he felt an urge to break free and run back to the safety of the home.

Sensing the boy's apprehension, Lucien released his grip on Trey's arm. "Almost there," he said in a hushed tone.

They turned left into a short corridor and approached the emergency exit at the back of the building. Trey could see that the electric wire linking the push-bar mechanism to the alarm had been cut, its two ends dangling beneath the machinery.

Lucien slowed slightly and, reaching into his top pocket, pulled out his sunglasses and placed them over his eyes. With his other hand he reached down to the umbrella that he was still carrying and released the pop-stud that had been keeping the material neatly twisted around the stem.

"What are you doing?" asked Trey incredulously. "It isn't raining outside, Lucien."

"I'm afraid that I have a rather rare skin complaint that does not allow me to come into direct contact with sunlight. It really is rather irksome, but if I don't take the necessary precautions, I'm afraid that the results are somewhat unpleasant." Kicking the push bar of the door with his left foot, he opened up the umbrella, ducked under its shade, and exited the building all in one swift movement.

Parked six feet away was a jet-black Lexus. With its heavily tinted, almost black, windows, Trey thought that it looked like some giant malevolent beetle just waiting to leap upon any unsuspecting victim that was foolish enough to roam too close to its waiting maw.

Lucien, who had kept the hand not carrying the umbrella firmly in his pocket since they had emerged from the building's interior, had depressed the key fob as they approached; the *chee-chook* sound of the alarm deactivating was followed by a satisfying clunk of the door locks being released.

"Front or back, Trey. I really do not care, but please be quick." Lucien approached the driver's door and Trey decided he would be more comfortable in the back. He hesitated, his fingers resting on the handle. He looked up at Lucien and, shaking his head at the stupidity of what he was about to do, opened the door and jumped into the backseat. He fastened his seat belt while looking out of the window to see what Lucien was doing. His heart pounded in his chest and he felt extremely hot and clammy, as the blood raced around his body carrying the fight-or-flight chemicals to every cell within it.

Outside, Lucien switched the umbrella to his left hand and, opening the door with the other, very quickly threw himself into the seat while simultaneously discarding the opened umbrella on the road outside the car and closing the door. For the first time since they had met, Trey saw that the man's impeccable self-composure had been allowed, momentarily, to slip. He was breathing hard and a slither of sweat snaked down the flesh on the back of his neck.

As Lucien sat in the seat for a minute to compose himself, Trey watched in horror as large, angry blisters started to form on the top of Lucien's head and the backs of his hands. They grew at an incredible rate, increasing their diameter five- or sixfold in the mere seconds that he watched, filling with a light yellowish-white fluid until the area around them looked pinched and sore. Trey had seen how quickly Lucien had entered the car and knew that those areas of skin could not have been exposed for more than a fraction of a second.

"Lucien, your skin . . . it's . . ."

He watched as the man in front of him gingerly touched the angry welts on the top of his head with the tips of his fingers. "I know. It's this . . . condition. I don't react very favorably to the sun. Don't worry, they'll be gone shortly."

"I don't think so. They look bad. You'll need a doctor. I think—"

"Trust me, Trey. I am an *extremely* fast healer." He removed the sunglasses and placed them on the passenger seat by his side. Starting the car, he began to pull away from the curb and away from the institution that had been Trey Laporte's home for the last three years. "Now, we need to make haste."

"This looks like a drug dealer's car," Trey remarked carelessly. In the rearview mirror he saw Lucien's cheeks rise and his eyes crinkle in what he guessed was a smile.

"Does it, indeed? Then I will certainly have to change it. The remote control for the television is in the lift-up compartment on your right. Feel free to watch what you like."

"I'm too wired to watch TV, Lucien. I think I'd just like to sit in peace for a while and try to work out what the hell I have just done."

Lucien nodded from the front, and they drove in silence for the remainder of the trip, mile after mile of countryside speeding past Trey's window as he gazed out from the rear of the car. He could feel his eyes start to drop and he blinked them open in frustration, shaking his head in disbelief that he could even consider the possibility of sleep after everything that had just happened. But the adrenaline dump that was taking place in his body right now was making him suddenly extremely weary. He felt his eyes blinking shut again and looked up to see Lucien regarding him in the rearview mirror.

"Sleep is a good thing," Lucien said. "We've got a long journey ahead of us, so, please, sleep as long as you like. You are quite safe now. Trust me."

Fighting the sudden waves of exhaustion that seemed to simply roll over him, Trey suddenly remembered that he had left the home without any of his possessions.

"My stuff . . ." he mumbled.

"Shhh, now. I will arrange for all of your personal items

to be collected by one of my people. Everything else—we will simply buy as new."

Trey looked around at the luxuriant car interior. "Are you rich, Lucien?" he asked.

"Yes. Disgustingly so."

"Where are we going?" His eyes fluttered as he fought to stay awake long enough to catch the answer.

"We are going to my apartment in London. You are coming to live with me, Mr. Laporte."

And with that, Trey gave himself up to the creeping sleep that encroached at the edges of his consciousness like some amorphous fog, and placed himself in the charge of Lucien Charron.

4

"Trey, wake up. We are here." Lucien was leaning back between the gap in the two front seats and gently shaking Trey out of the sleep he was in.

"Unghh, where are we?" Trey said. His neck ached from the uncomfortable sleeping position that he had adopted against the car door. He opened his eyes and looked out of the window onto a bleak open space of concrete pillars and sickly colored fluorescent lighting. Twenty or so cars were parked in various bays, their colors difficult to make out under the garish green hue of the strip lights.

"We're in the underground parking lot beneath my apartment block. You've slept the entire journey here," Lucien said.

"I'm sorry . . ."

"Please, there is no need to apologize. You have been through an awful lot in such a short space of time, it's understandable that your mind would want to rest. Come along." Lucien climbed out of the front seat. He moved around the outside of the car; then, like a chauffeur, he deferentially swung back the rear door on Trey's side and made a grand sweeping gesture with his other arm. "Your new home awaits."

Trey climbed out, suddenly feeling very wary of his surroundings. The underground parking lot smelled of acrid
exhaust fumes, and even the smallest sound was transformed into a harsh echo as it bounced around the walls.
The sickly feeling of fear welled up within him again as
the stupidity of his actions suddenly crushed in on him. He
jumped slightly at the sound of the car locking behind him,
but if Lucien spotted this, he didn't comment. He simply
turned his back on the boy and walked toward an elevator
set into a wall on their right.

"Do come along, Trey," Lucien said over his shoulder,
pressing a small button in the wall next to the doors. "We
live on the top floor."

Trey walked over to the doors as they slid open. His mind
slowly cleared of the sleepy fog that had dulled it moments
before. He was fully alert again now and on edge as he got
into the small elevator compartment. Lucien stabbed at the
uppermost button, and the doors slid shut on the pair.

"I am guessing that you are hungry?" Lucien said.

Trey hadn't even thought of food, but the mere mention of it caused his stomach to groan noisily and twist as
though some parasitic beast living within him had suddenly
been awakened. "Ravenous. I could eat a horse with a soup
spoon . . . but I feel sick at the same time," Trey replied.
The tall man next to him laughed for the first time since
they had met. It was a deep, wonderful sound that seemed
completely at odds coming from such a stern, alarming-
looking individual. Trey found himself smiling in spite of

the creeping worry-worm that wriggled and gnawed away inside of him.

He's not what he says he is, the worm whispered. Run now while you still have a chance.

"Well, I can't promise any horse tonight, but I am sure that we can find something that will satisfy your appetite."

The elevator finished its ascent, the metal doors sliding open to reveal Lucien's apartment. Trey stood in the opening and stared, wide-eyed, at the opulence of the room before him. It was a huge room that he guessed must have been at least forty meters in length. The white walls were crowned with a dark blue glass suspended ceiling that hung impossibly above the entire space and reflected back an image of it in its surface. Rugs broke up the expanse of cream carpeting that stretched from the elevator to the far side of the room, where huge floor-to-ceiling windows allowed the last of the early evening sunlight in, filling it with a golden hue. Trey could see the towering form of Canary Wharf rising behind some of the buildings that faced them from across the other side of the river. Everything inside the apartment was so *big*. Three doors were uniformly arranged along both side walls, which, in turn, were lavishly adorned with works of art and tapestries. Trey's eyes were drawn to a giant tapestry in the center of one wall: The scene sewn into its surface in silken thread showed mounted huntsmen who had cornered a white stag. A lance pierced the animal's heart; the creature's head was twisted in agony as it died at its pursuers' hands.

In the center of the room, encircled by large obsidian

stones, burned a log fire, its smoke being gobbled up by a polished metal hood hanging from a suspended column in the ceiling.

Standing next to the fire, perfectly still and upright, was a tall, powerful-looking man. A large unsightly scar dominated the right side of his face, and it appeared to have healed poorly, the scar tissue pulling the flesh in on itself, giving it an ugly, puckered appearance. His hair was black, with hints of gray, and was cropped close to his head, lending him a distinctly military air. He was wearing a dark blue suit that, like Lucien's, looked expensive, the cut of his clothing enhancing his muscular frame. He nodded at Trey, his head barely dipping in acknowledgment, before his gaze turned back to Lucien.

"Welcome back, Lucien." The man spoke in a broad Irish accent. He strode across the room toward them, crossing the threshold of the elevator, and Trey had to stop himself from taking a step backward in response.

"Nice to meet you, young man," he said in a voice that sounded as if he gargled with bleach every morning. He held out a hand in greeting.

Trey wasn't at all surprised to find that the man's hands were tough and callused: hands that had been used for hard work. He was, however, surprised by the warmth of the handshake, as his hand was gripped firmly and covered by the man's other hand.

"Trey, this is Thomas," Lucien announced, looking from one to the other. "He is my right-hand man and he helps, among a whole host of other things, to keep my businesses running smoothly when my attentions are elsewhere. He'll do his best to make sure you are comfortable here, and if there is anything you need, I'm sure that Thomas would be happy to try to get it for you."

"You call me Tom," the Irishman said, glancing at the other man from under his eyebrows. "Thomas indeed! The first thing that'll start to infuriate you about this great long streak of I-don't-know-what is his unrelenting formality." He released Trey's hand and stepped back, cocking his head to one side, his eyebrows raised high as if expecting an answer to some unspoken question. When none came, he turned his back on them, walking away and shouting over his shoulder, "Well, are the two of you coming in, or are you going to stand in the lift all night like a couple of *eejits*? I suppose you'll both be wanting something to eat?" He disappeared into the farthest door set into the right-hand wall.

Lucien ushered Trey into the room and gestured toward a brown leather recliner facing the fire. "Make yourself at home, Trey. I shall go and ascertain what culinary delights our housekeeper, Mrs. Magilton, has left for us. If you'd like to watch something on the television, feel free." He bent down toward the chair and picked up a remote control with a large blue LCD display which he handed to Trey. "If you press this button," he continued, "the TV slides up out of the floor over there." He gestured to an area on Trey's left. "Beyond that, I really don't have a clue how it works, but

I'm sure that you'll work it out in no time." He smiled and exited through the same door that Tom had just used, leaving Trey on his own.

Trey watched him leave before staring around again at his fabulous surroundings. The place screamed of money. Big money. It wouldn't have looked out of place on a show he had seen on MTV about the houses of famous athletes and rap stars. He couldn't imagine how anybody could accrue enough money to live in this kind of luxury, and he thought back to his comment to Lucien when they had first got into the Lexus about it looking like a drug dealer's car. Lucien had smiled at the remark and quipped about changing it. But if not drugs, what? The worry-worm returned, forcing its way through the soft tissues of his brain, churning up the fears and doubts that he had hitherto fought to suppress.

Maybe Lucien was a gangster of some kind? Maybe he was involved in organized crime. Both he and Tom looked like the type: hard men who wouldn't think twice about using violence to get what they wanted. Trey shook his head in disbelief. He'd allowed himself to run away with a man that he knew nothing about and he'd based that decision on *what*? Some misguided trust in somebody because he had claimed to know his parents. The thought that Trey had tried to bury for so long now finally rose up and lodged itself firmly in his mind. Maybe Lucien was some kind of child killer? Maybe he'd built his wealth on selling teenage boys to people who did terrible things to them?

Trey looked down at the remote he was holding. His hands were shaking so badly that he could hardly keep hold of the thing as he struggled to control his rising anxiety. For want of something to do, he pressed the button that Lucien had indicated, and the largest television he'd ever seen slid silently up out of the floor and turned itself on. One of the countless celebrity chefs that seemed to be forever on the TV was demonstrating how to make some kind of salmon terrine. The sound of his voice seemed to come from all around the room and Trey glanced about him to see if he could locate the hidden speakers. He pressed the same button again, and the giant screen obeyed his command by going into standby mode and silently sliding back into its hiding place in the floor.

He stood and walked across the room on shaking legs and took in the view out of the window. He was high up. He had neglected to notice the floor number that the apartment was on, but one look through the window was enough to tell him that he was near the top of a very tall building. He looked around again, searching the room for a way in or out except for the elevator. Surely there must be a fire exit? He wanted to be certain that he could still escape this place if he needed to.

He jumped slightly as the door next to him opened again. Lucien stood there, looking quizzically at the boy.

"Is everything OK?" he asked, inclining his head to one side. He was drying his hands on a white tea towel, and as he finished, Trey noticed that the ugly blisters that had come up on them earlier had completely disappeared. He switched his attention to the top of Lucien's head and noticed that this too was completely free of the angry marks that he had witnessed form all over the bald dome.

"Your hands," he said, nodding toward the flesh where, only hours earlier, there had been a mass of angry pus-filled burns.

Lucien glanced down at the area that Trey was staring at. He smiled awkwardly and shrugged his shoulders. "I told you, Trey, I am a very quick healer. Now, if you would like to . . ."

Trey looked up into those alien eyes again. A small gasp escaped him as all of the fears and doubts and feelings he had harbored about this stranger suddenly crushed in on him. He backed away from him, catching his heel on one of the rugs as he did so, and stumbled, but quickly regained his footing. He felt as if he was moving through treacle, his limbs not responding to his commands to get as far away from this man as possible. He kept his eyes locked on Lucien, who remained in the doorway, and desperately tried to remember the layout of the room as he retreated toward the elevator doors on the other side.

Lucien followed the boy with eyes that reflected nothing but concern. "Trey, are you all right?" he asked. "If it's about the blisters, I can explain. Maybe you thought they were worse than they really were. You were tired and—"

Trey found it difficult to control his voice—it trembled and quivered as he spoke. "No. I know what I saw earlier. I watched your skin erupt in great angry blisters that should have taken days or weeks to heal. And that happened because you exposed yourself to the sun for a fraction of a second, Lucien." He thought back to the moment that Lucien had stared into the eyes of Colin Wallington and seemed to *see* into his inner secrets. He thought of how the world had seemed to stop when he had done this. But most of all, he thought of the dead fly and how it had appeared to come back to life as soon as Lucien's mood had changed, having bent Colin's will to his own.

He should have run from the room at the care home then. He should have got as far away from this . . . *thing* as he could when he had the chance.

The dangers that Lucien had alluded to earlier that morning were clear and present all right. Trey had just been too brainless to realize that they had been standing right in front of him all along.

Trey's back finally met with the wall at the far end of the room and his hand crabbed its way along the surface behind him, trying to locate the elevator button. He rested his finger against it, the flat pad of his finger pressing lightly against the resistance afforded by the switch without fully engaging the mechanism to call the lift. Even now, with fear filling every part of his being, he couldn't bring himself to call upon the only means of escape available to him.

Why was that? Why didn't he obey the part of him

that bellowed inside him to get away? He shook his head, frowning at his inability to act. *Because you want to know for certain, Trey,* the niggling voice of the worry-worm inside his head chided. *Because you want to know if what you believe about him is really true. And because, despite your fear, you still believe that he can tell you things about yourself and your parents that you* need *to know.*

Trey could not remember seeing Lucien move away from the kitchen door and cross the room toward him. Yet the man stood no more than a few meters away from him now, still wearing that look of concern and pity that he had throughout.

Trey's hands were shaking so badly that they slipped off the elevator button and he frantically sought to locate it again.

An image appeared in his mind's eye. A perfect freeze-frame image of the little black fly lying on its back on the windowsill.

He looked up at the man again and fought to keep his voice under control. "Your . . . skin complaint," he said, ignoring the catch in his voice that made it difficult for him to get the words out properly. "I take it that you've had it for a long time?"

"All my life."

"So you can only go out safely at night then? You can't be exposed to sunlight?'

"That's correct, Trey," Lucien responded. A sad smile played momentarily at the edges of his mouth. "But you

50

had already worked that out, hadn't you? You are a bright lad, but you've been battling against your instincts since we met. Why? Why won't you listen to that inner voice of yours and ask me the question that is really bothering you?"

"And what is that, Lucien?" Trey's voice sounded alien to his own ears, as though he were merely mouthing the words and someone else inhabited his body at that moment.

"Do I really need to tell you? Is hearing it from my lips the only way that you can believe what your instincts are telling you about *what* I am?"

Trey wavered slightly. His vision had gone somewhat out of focus and dark objects danced around in front of his eyes. He willed himself to breathe, but his lungs refused to obey. "Maybe that's it. Maybe I have to hear you say it." He struggled to get these words out. His shaking finger accidentally depressed the button behind him fully and he could hear the elevator engine hum quietly into life as it ascended from a lower floor.

Lucien stared at Trey with those odd, frightening eyes for what seemed like an age, before finally nodding the smallest of nods.

"I'm a vampire, Trey. A night-stalker. Undead. A nether-creature."

Trey's peripheral vision had all but gone completely now, replaced by a gray curtain that obscured everything not directly in front of him in a thick fog. He tried to speak, but no words would come. His knees buckled slightly, and the effect was enough to make him stagger forward a step, just as the elevator door behind him announced its arrival with a soft pinging sound. He reached out to grab ahold of something that wasn't there, his hands closing around nothing but the air in front of him, and he collapsed into the thick shag carpet.

Lucien called for Tom as he knelt down next to Trey.

"What's happened?" the Irishman asked as he hurried across the room to help.

"He's fainted," Lucien said.

"Fainted?"

"He collapsed. I think a combination of the lack of food coupled with the realization that you have run away with a vampire would cause most people to pass out." He looked up at Tom and sighed. "I had wished to explain all of this to him in a more . . . controlled manner. I think that we should move Trey to his room so that he will be more comfortable."

He stood up and effortlessly lifted Trey's unconscious body in his arms. He followed Tom across the room and through the farthest door on the left, where they gently placed Trey on a bed, exchanging concerned looks as they stood back from the prone figure.

Tom quietly pulled the door closed behind them and turned to look over at his vampire boss. "Do you think he will be all right?" he asked.

Lucien shook his head and cast his eyes toward the

door. "I sincerely hope so, Tom, because young Mr. Laporte is going to need every ounce of strength to survive what lies ahead of him in the next few days and weeks."

5

Trey opened his eyes. He took in the details of the strange ceiling overhead and remembered where he was. He slowly turned his head and stopped, the breath catching in his throat when he saw the girl sitting in the chair next to his bed. She was looking down and reading the book held in her lap.

Even though she was sitting, it was clear that she was tall, with long black hair that hung down her back in a ponytail. She was dressed in a gray-striped top under a shiny black waistcoat, with a short gray skirt and black leggings. Her makeup was in a Goth style, and, while it had not been applied too harshly, Trey thought that it seemed to spoil the soft lines of her heart-shaped face. It was clear to him that, despite the makeup, she was painfully pretty—maybe even beautiful. He guessed she was about sixteen years old.

As if aware of his scrutiny for the first time, she folded the corner of the page that she was on and closed the book before lifting her face to look at him. She examined his face for a moment before revealing her perfect teeth in a broad smile.

"You must be Trey," she said casually. "My father has told me an awful lot about you."

"Well, that's a whole lot more than he's told me," he

replied, immediately regretting the petulant tone in his voice. He knew from the intensity of her eyes that she must be Lucien's daughter.

There was a pause, during which she nodded thoughtfully. "This must all seem like the weirdest day of your life at the moment, huh?" she said. "Running away from that care home with some guy that you've never met before—that's pretty hard-core. Then you find out that this *guy* is a vampire . . ." She puffed out her cheeks. "You must feel that your entire universe has been turned on its head right now." She nodded her head again and smiled at him in a way that Trey assumed was a look of admiration. He held her eyes and tried to look braver than he really felt.

If only you knew, he thought.

His heart had taken up the fluttery arrhythmia that he had almost become accustomed to now, and the familiar feeling of dread began to creep its way through him again. He sat up on the bed and swung his legs over the side so that he faced her.

She leaned forward slightly, lowering her voice. "You know, despite everything that you are probably thinking to the contrary, you have to believe him when he says that he has been looking out for your interests for a very long time and that he has things to tell you that are truly important for you to understand about yourself."

"He hasn't really told me anything. Just that he knew my parents and that I'm in danger," Trey said. He gave up trying to sound tough and aloof, and his voice sounded high and fragile to his own ears.

"You're safe now that you are here with us. I think that Lucien's just really unsure of how to begin telling you everything. He's very worried about how you'll react."

Trey shook his head at this, a hot anger building up inside of him. How was it that these people presumed to know so much about him, and *why* were they not willing to simply tell him what was going on?

Before he could reply, there was a knock at the door. When it opened, Lucien's face was revealed in the gap. "Ah, wonderful! You're awake, Trey. And the two of you have met."

"Not really, Dad. Trey's literally only just come round," the girl replied, smiling warmly at him.

"Then allow me to make the introductions. Trey Laporte, this is my daughter, Alexa Charron. Alexa, this is Trey." He looked sheepishly over in Trey's direction. "Tom has made some tea," he said, as if everything that had happened to Trey that day would be set right by the hot drink. "And there is food, if you feel up to eating something. I would recommend that you do—we don't want you keeling over like that again." He looked at his daughter again and smiled. "Alexa, I'm sure that Trey would appreciate a quick tour of his new home before we sit down for dinner. Perhaps you'd be so kind as to show him around?" He nodded in Trey's direction and closed the door.

Trey looked at the closed door in disbelief. Clearly,

56

revealing that you were a vampire did not rate highly on Lucien Charron's list of things to freak you out. Sensing his mood, Alexa leaned forward and placed her hand on his arm.

"Let go of me," Trey said, pulling free of Alexa. He tried to get to his feet and almost fell over again as the blood rushed to his head. Regaining his balance, he looked about him frantically, wondering what he was going to do.

"Take it easy, Trey. You passed out. My father carried you into your room—sorry, the room that will be yours, if you choose to stay here with us—so that you could lie down."

His head spun as his brain raced through scenarios and possible outcomes of the situation he now found himself in. He had willingly *allowed* himself to be brought here to this place, despite a growing feeling that something was very wrong about the whole thing. The man called Lucien had freely admitted to him that he was a vampire, and now it seemed that he had been drugged and brought here to this room while the vampire's daughter sat guard over him to ensure he could not escape.

What have I done? How could I have been so stupid? I'm going to die, and I led myself into this like some lamb to the slaughter.

He needed to get out of here. Get away from this apartment and let the authorities know what was going on here. The moment he considered this, he realized how stupid an idea it was. What would he tell the police? That there

57

was a vampire living in this apartment in Docklands? OK, he didn't have fangs, or claws, or wear a cloak and walk around saying, "I vant to suck your blut." But he was a vampire nevertheless. He could almost hear the police laughing him out of the station.

"Do you want to just sit down and talk about things?" Alexa said from the chair. She watched as he began to rifle through the drawer of a small cabinet that stood in a corner of the room. "What are you looking for, Trey?" Alexa asked.

"Something to protect myself with. A knife, scissors, anything," he mumbled to himself. He shook his head in desperation at the neatly folded stacks of bedclothes and towels that were housed in the drawers. There was nothing even remotely like a weapon in sight.

"Are you sure that you've really thought this through? Exactly what is it that you are so worried about?" Her calm, unflustered tone sounded completely at odds with his own feelings as his thoughts and emotions scrambled over each other in an effort to try to make sense of things.

He ignored her, and his eyes fell upon a small, silver-handled letter opener on top of the bureau. He picked it up and hefted it in his hand. He tried to imagine standing in front of Lucien or Tom, brandishing this small, effete tool in their faces as a warning. A small whimper escaped him as the hopelessness of his situation dawned on him.

"Trey," Alexa said, "why are you freaking out?"

He stopped for a moment and turned to her with a look of utter disbelief. "Are you insane?" he said. "Your dad is going to *eat* me! That's why I'm *freaking out*!"

"Think about it," Alexa said, getting up and taking a step toward him. "If my father had wanted to harm you in any way—which is quite the opposite of his intentions— couldn't he easily have done so at any point without bringing you back here to our house to do so?"

He turned to look up at her.

She held his eyes with her own, her stare open and frank. "I think you already knew," she said quietly. "Perhaps you weren't absolutely certain, but I think that you had a good idea about what my father really is," she continued.

"That's absurd. How could I possibly have known?"

"Maybe you have talents and senses that you choose not to recognize," she said, giving a little shrug of her shoulders. "I don't know, maybe you're not as 'normal' as you'd like to think. Have you ever felt that, Trey? Felt that you aren't like the other people around you?"

He paused, taking a deep breath and considering what she had just said. He found both her tone and the question unsettling. Had he known? Had he somehow guessed in that moment that Lucien had removed his sunglasses to look at him that he was not human?

"I have no idea what the hell you are talking about. Lucien is a vampire. Why would I willingly put myself into the hands of something like that?"

"Because maybe you feel that you and he are not so

59

different after all?" Alexa raised one eyebrow and tilted her head slightly to one side. It was an action, Trey thought, that made her look even more attractive, and he was once again struck by just how pretty she really was.

What am I thinking? This was Lucien's daughter. Lucien Charron, who had calmly admitted to being a fully paid-up member of the undead. And here he was, eyeing her up, when only seconds ago he'd been imagining her father tearing his throat open to feast on his blood. He stopped and looked at her suspiciously, his heart smashing against his rib cage.

She was his daughter, so she must be one too.

He stood up and backed away, holding the pathetic letter opener in front of him in one hand.

"You're hypnotizing me right now, aren't you? That's what you do, isn't it? Vampires put their victims in a kind of trance. I'm not thinking straight because you've hypnotized me and later on you're all going to feast on me!" The words spewed from his mouth and he heard the hysteria rising in his voice. He had to concentrate to stop the hand holding the letter opener from shaking too violently.

A small smile played on her lips and she raised her hands in front of her as if to show him that she was of no threat to him. "I'm not hypnotizing you, Trey, and I am not a vampire." She kept her hands held out in front of her, and stepped to her right to stand directly in front of a large freestanding mirror. She turned so that she faced him in the mirror's surface, holding his eyes with hers. "See?" she said, indicating the image in the silvered glass with a brief nod of her head. "Reflection in the mirror. You *do* know that vampires don't have reflections in mirrors, don't you?" With a soft sigh she turned back to face him, fixing his eyes with her own.

"I'm a halfling. My mother was a human, I have never fed upon the blood of a vampire, so I am neither undead or encumbered with all of the . . . difficulties *that my father has to deal with."*

Trey could hear the sound of her voice as clearly as if she had walked up and whispered in his ear, but her lips had not moved. He felt a gentle kind of *pushing* at his subconscious, not unpleasant and not at all threatening. He blinked, trying to take this in as her voice continued in his mind.

"My father has put himself at considerable risk to save you today, Trey. He has exposed himself to forces and people that, even now, will be using their power to find you and kill you. If he had not acted when he did, there is every chance that you would by now be dead. He has the answers to questions that you do not yet even know you need to ask. And all we request in return is that you listen to these things before you make up your mind about us and about what you want to do."

Under and between these words were swirling layers of overlapping color that wove in and out of them. He felt safe, as though he were a small child being enveloped in a warm, soft blanket. He had no doubt that she was using some kind of magic on him to keep him from losing it completely, but, despite this, he was strangely calmed, grateful even, for the brake that she had applied to the panic that had threatened to carry him away with it.

"You're hypnotizing me *now*, aren't you?" Trey said in a small voice.

"Kind of," Alexa answered, speaking again now. "I wanted you to calm down quickly before you keeled over and hurt yourself. You really do need to think about breathing a little more often." She smiled at him, and he felt himself smiling back.

"You're telling me that I'm not in any danger," Trey stammered. "Is that right? That despite all this madness—vampires, magic, revelations about myself—I'm not in any *immediate* danger."

"About the only imminent danger that you are in tonight is having to face one of Mrs. Magilton's meals. She tries very hard, but she simply isn't a very good cook. Dad's too soft and refuses to let her go. She only does one dish particularly well and that's cottage pie. And there is only so much minced beef and mashed potato that anyone can stand." She did that thing that she did when she cocked her head to one side again, and Trey felt himself reddening.

"Stick with it for a little while longer, Trey. If you don't get any satisfactory answers and you still think that you're in peril here, all you have to do is ask to leave and my father will take you anywhere that you want to go. If you don't want my father to take you anywhere, Tom or I would be happy to help—we are neither of us bloodsucking fiends, as you'd put it."

Trey held her gaze as though he might be able to find something in her eyes to belie what she had just told him. Eventually he nodded and lowered the weapon that he had been brandishing toward her throughout this exchange. He looked down at the small tool in his hand and flushed red again with the realization of just how utterly pathetic he must have looked waving it around.

She was still standing with her back to the mirror, a sly, coquettish look on her face, and he found himself imagining what it would be like to kiss her on the lips.

"Wouldn't you like to know?" came that intimate whisper in his ear, and he could no longer bear to look her in the eye as his face burned crimson red.

"Your bathroom is through there," she said, indicating a sliding door on his right. "And there's a walk-in wardrobe through that archway over there. Unfortunately, Tom picked out the clothes we got for you. Mostly skate wear with some sports gear thrown in that he thought you'd like. Actually, there are some pretty cool jeans in there and a hoodie that I've got my eye on if you don't want it." She smiled before turning her back on him and moving toward the door. She added, over her shoulder, "As Dad said, we can go out soon and you can pick yourself a whole load of stuff to your own liking. I know some great shops in London that I bet you'll love."

He watched her as she started to leave the room.

"Just one thing, Alexa." Trey called after her, and she stopped in the opening, turning toward him again. "That mind-speaking thing you do—how did you learn that?"

"My mother was a sorceress. Before she died, when I was young, she started to teach me magecraft. I've carried on learning from books and the people that work for my father. I'm pretty good, if I say so myself."

"Can I ask you not to read my mind anymore? I'm not comfortable with it."

Alexa laughed and gently shook her head at him. "I can't *read* minds, Trey. I'm nowhere near *that* good yet. It's just a simple thought-transfer spell. It's all one-way traffic, I'm afraid."

"But earlier, when you said, 'Wouldn't you like to know?' how did you know—"

"Trey," she interrupted, "when a boy stares at a girl's lips and starts licking his own, it's really not too difficult to work out what he's thinking." She turned and went to leave, stopping one more time. "Like I said, just try to hang in there. We'll see you in the kitchen for dinner when you feel good and ready. Take your time." She gave him a little wave and added with a playful smile, "Oh, and if you're going to hang around here for a while, it might pay to learn the correct terminology. Vampires don't *eat* people, they tear their throats out and mercilessly drain them of their blood. And the mirror thing? Rubbish. All vamps have reflections. Why wouldn't they?" She winked at him, before finally leaving and pushing the door shut.

Trey looked at the back of the closed door. Despite everything, he found himself smiling again and he resolved to at least listen to what Lucien was so determined he should tell him.

He walked into the bathroom that was bigger than his entire bedroom back at the home. Stepping into the shower, he stood beneath the hot jets of water and allowed the day's grime to be washed away from him, toying with the silver amulet that hung around his neck. He had to force himself not to dwell too much on what had happened so far that day, redirecting his thoughts to more neutral and pleasant things, because when he didn't, fresh floods of panic and doubt roared through him, convincing him that he was insane to still be there. No, he'd listen to what they had to say and then make up his mind what he would do.

When he had finished in the bathroom, he quickly dressed, putting on some of the clothes that Tom had bought him, and left the room on shaking legs to eat with his new hosts.

6

They had sat down to eat around a large circular table next to the kitchen area. Dinner consisted of a fish and seafood stew that Trey actually thought was one of the best things he'd ever eaten. Alexa kept him at ease, asking him about his life in the care facility and how he had coped with living there. He surprised himself by eating the entire plate of food, losing himself in the conversation, and briefly managing to shut out most of the nagging thoughts that nibbled away at him whenever he allowed his mind to wander.

The vast floor-to-ceiling windows that filled the south wall of the main room extended along the same wall in the kitchen, and Lucien sat staring through these at the dark waters of the river Thames throughout most of the meal, hardly touching his food. Trey kept stealing glances at him, and each time he did, his heart quickened and banged against its bony enclosure as he thought about the creature that he was sharing the table with. He wondered at how this had all come about. He was a normal boy living a normal, if some-what dull, life and suddenly he was sitting around a table with a vampire, his *halfling* daughter and a man who looked like he would quite happily reach across the table and gut him with his dinner knife without thinking twice about it.

Keep it together, Trey, he told himself, and thought about what Alexa had said to him before dinner.

A silence descended upon the room once everyone had finished eating, and Trey couldn't help but notice that it was Lucien who looked the most concerned and distracted of the people sitting around the table. The worry-worm wriggled and squirmed again, burrowing into the tiny island of calm he had managed to create for himself. He began to imagine what it was that Lucien had to tell him that was causing a creature like a *vampire* to look so worried.

"Do you like football?" Tom asked, cutting through the silence and speaking for the first time during the entire meal.

"I beg your pardon?" Trey replied, completely taken aback by the question that seemed so utterly at odds with the situation.

"Which team do you support?"

"Tottenham Hotspur."

"Humph," snorted Tom. "Celtic. Now there's a *proper* football team. Best bloody football team in the country."

Trey considered backing down. He certainly didn't want to upset the man with the ugly scar sitting opposite him, but he had been through enough already today, and something stirred inside him that made him answer back with a firmness in his voice that he had stifled until now.

"Actually, I don't think they'd make it in the Premiership. I think that if they ever got a chance to play in England, they'd struggle against a lot of Championship sides."

Tom looked over at him. The hard stare that Trey faced was particularly unpleasant, and he had a tough time meeting it. Suddenly, Tom's face broke into a smile. It was a lopsided affair, the ruined side of his face lacking some of the muscles needed to complete their part of the task, so the end result was a half smile, half grimace that was none too appealing.

"Maybe I'll take you up there one day—that's if you're sticking around, of course—show you just how good they really are." He stood up and picked up his plate, reaching over for Trey's and collecting Alexa's and Lucien's in turn.

"I'd like that. But only if we get to go to Tottenham afterward, so that you can see a proper team play." Trey smiled back at him and received a wink from the tall Irishman before he turned his back and stepped up into the kitchen area to load the dishes into the dishwasher.

"Shall we move to the reading room?" Lucien said, standing up from the table. "I think it's time for me to tell you some of those things that I promised to, Trey." He looked over at Tom, who was on his haunches, loading crockery into the racks of the machine. "Will you join us, Tom?"

"I'll be right through, Lucien, as soon as I've got rid of the worst of this. You go ahead."

They retired to a small, book-lined room that was accessed from the main living room. It was, in comparison to the other rooms in the apartment, relatively small. There were no windows, but a skylight in the ceiling revealed the night sky above their heads, the light from long-dead stars winking at them. Artificial light was provided by elegant swan-necked lamps that hung from the walls. Three tall curved reading lamps—their shades hanging over the chairs like snooping neighbors peering over the garden fence—were also in the room, but these were not turned on yet. Trey looked over at the studded leather door set into the farthest wall and wondered what lay beyond.

The walls were filled with high bookshelves, and Trey guessed that the majority of the books were incredibly old. Two comfortable-looking black sofas faced each other across a smoked-glass coffee table, empty except for one of the ancient volumes that lay facedown in the center.

Lucien sat down on the nearest sofa and gestured for his daughter and Trey to sit on the other. He sighed as he allowed his back to merge with the soft leather cushion behind him. Steepling his hands together, he gently tapped the backs of his thumbs against his bottom lip, unwilling or uncertain how to begin the task ahead of him.

"I want to ask you how much you know about yourself, Trey," he said after a long pause. "But that would be entirely unfair of me after I have promised you answers and not questions. So I shall start by telling you some things about who you are and what you are, and you can fill in any gaps. Is that OK?" he asked, a sympathetic look on his face.

"As I have already told you, I knew your mother and father, and I deeply respected and . . . loved them both. Your father and I shared certain . . . skills and interests, and we used these resources to try to do some good in the world."

He stopped and smiled at Trey. "Your father, Daniel, was a great man, and you should feel hugely proud about the difference that he made to a great number of people's lives. I will provide you with the means to find out very much more about your parents, especially your father and the work that he did, so that you can understand a little better where you come from."

"He was an architect," Trey interrupted.

"No, Trey. Your father was not an architect. He did help to build great things, but he did that by fighting against those who would have anything decent and virtuous in this world reduced to pain and filth and misery. Ultimately this struggle led to his untimely death, but before this he was nothing less than a brilliant beacon that was never afraid to cast its light and fire into the darkness that threatens us all."

"Lucien, you're not making any sense. What is this all about?" Trey asked.

"There are people, and *things*, in this world who constantly strive to destroy everything that you and I would consider good. Pitched against them are those like your father, who, in spite of the awesome power of the enemy, are committed to obstructing them in their quest."

Tom quietly entered the room and sat on the arm of the sofa.

Lucien continued. "We in this room are committed to continuing the struggle that your father gave his life for. Like your father, we use our gifts and powers to try to stem the evil that others would unleash upon humanity. Trey, we would like you to join us."

Trey looked at the people around him. The grave looks upon their faces merely added to how he felt about the utter ludicrousness of what he was hearing. "Are you all mad? Or is it me that has completely come off the rails?" he said, getting to his feet. "First you tell me that you're a vampire, Alexa appears to have hypnotized me in some way to make me believe in telepathy, and now you're banging on about some titanic struggle between good and evil that you and my father were involved in. Then . . . then you sit there straight-faced and tell me that you want me to *join* you! This is insane, Lucien! I'm just a fourteen-year-old kid, who, until today, didn't believe in vampires and whose only experience of them was exterminating them on his games console!"

Lucien stood and faced Trey, his eyes scanning the boy's face. "No, Trey, you're not just some fourteen-year-old kid—not after last night. Because, last night, although you have no memory of it, you experienced for the first time the full revelation of what you really are. You are a lycanthrope: a werewolf."

Trey stood there, his mouth hanging wide-open as he shook his head in bewildered disbelief. "Yeah, yeah, of course I am," he said eventually, his voice dripping with sarcasm. "I'm a werewolf, you and her are vampires, and I suppose old Tom over there is a zombie or something, eh?"

"Zombie, indeed!" Tom responded. "I wouldn't wipe my

arse with zombies. Dirty, stupid, foul creatures they are—too stupid to know that they should stay dead. I'm one hundred percent human and just you remember that. And less of the old, you cheeky little git."

Lucien looked over at Tom, stopping the other man saying more before continuing: "It's true, Trey. You are the child of werewolf parents. That makes you incredibly rare. We believe that you might be the last *hereditary werewolf* in existence—meaning that you inherited the condition, as opposed to those who actively seek to become werewolves or those who survive an attack. As such, you have tremendous inborn powers, but now that these have become manifest, there are huge dangers that threaten your very existence, and—"

"Madness," Trey interrupted, still shaking his head. "If I *was* a werewolf—*which* I am not—how do you explain that I have never run out in the middle of the night and howled at a full moon, or woken up in a forest somewhere after tearing out the throat of some poor unsuspecting virgin? Surely even a very young werewolf must be a bit of a handful when he is growing up?"

"A male lycanthrope can only transform from the human form to the wolf form when the levels of testosterone in his body rise above a certain level," Alexa said. "Before that, there are very few signs of what he will become. In changing from a boy to a man, the wolf that has lain dormant inside you for so long has been released."

"Last night you transmogrified for the first time," Lucien

explained. "Luckily, you were alone in your room at the time, or I shudder to think what the consequences might have been. As I have explained to you, Trey, I have been keeping a careful and watchful eye on you ever since your parents died, and had hoped that I might be able to intercede before this moment came. Unfortunately, that was not possible and I am deeply sorry for what happened to you yesterday evening. I take full responsibility and hope that you can forgive me."

"What *did* happen to me?" Trey's voice sounded thin and papery inside his head. "Please God, tell me that I didn't kill anybody."

"No, of course you didn't." Lucien reached out a hand to touch the boy, but instinctively drew it back, aware of how fragile he seemed. "We would not have allowed such a thing to happen to you, Trey. Tom's people have had the care home under constant surveillance since you were moved there three years ago. Our man was alerted as to what might happen yesterday night by Alexa—she has certain gifts that allow her to 'tune in' to unusual occurrences—werewolves, vampires, demons, all nether-creatures produce a signal when they are on the human plane, and Alexa picked up yours. Tom's man witnessed the whole thing and ensured that no harm came to you or anybody else. You simply broke free from your room and roamed around for a few hours before returning a little after four in the morning. We were able to keep track of you throughout—Tom's people are very thorough."

Lucien took a deep breath and went on: "You should know that there are two states of lycanthropy. The first, and by far the most dangerous to the shape-shifter himself, is the Wolfan. When the lycanthrope changes into this form, all vestiges of his humanity are lost to him. He becomes a giant wolf, an incredibly powerful monster with an evil desire to kill, often hunting down his prey and murdering it in horrific fashion. Each time the lycanthrope adopts this form, his beast aspect grows in power and influence until it consumes him. He is then cursed to be subject to the control of the full moon forever and to obey the evil that has been sown within him. The Wolfan is the *normal* lycanthropic state."

"The other form," Alexa said, taking over from her father, "is known as bimorphism. This is when the lycanthrope changes into a half-man, half-wolf creature. He stands upright like a man, but his body is otherwise that of a wolf. He maintains his thought processes and intelligence, and wields a greater control over the more base urges within him. He will have superhuman strength as well as acute senses of hearing, sight, and smell—which may take the form of synesthesia . . ."

"What on earth is that?" asked Trey.

"It's a condition where smells are perceived as colors or sounds," Lucien explained, before allowing Alexa to continue.

"He will have extraordinary powers of rejuvenation, making you—sorry, him—almost impossible to kill, and unlike those lycanthropes who have succumbed to the Wolfan, he will have the ability to change shape voluntarily, regardless of whether it is day or night, or indeed what phase the moon may be in."

Trey pictured the chaos that he had woken up to in his room that morning. It had occurred to him at the time how much force it must have taken to destroy his sneakers so utterly. And then there were the gouges in the metal frame of the window and the plaster walls.

A small icy shiver ran down his spine.

"The amulet that I gave you was worn by your father." Lucien's voice broke through his thoughts. "It is an ancient talisman that contains wolfsbane and can help the wearer control the transformation process. Moreover, its wearer will only ever transform into the bimorphic werewolf state that Alexa described, thus retaining his human faculties and intellect." He paused and held the teenager's stare. "It cannot stop all involuntary changes that might occur when you feel extremely threatened or angry, but it allows you to control the condition that you have inherited from birth."

"I'll get us some tea," said Tom, standing up and exiting the room.

"Is there a . . . cure?" Trey asked.

"No. You don't have a disease, Trey, although right now it must seem very much as if you do. But this is what you are. You're a werewolf, and you will need to learn to cope with that."

Trey looked at the faces of the two people left in the room with him, searching for some tiny signal that this was some kind of joke.

"A werewolf," he eventually said. "How . . . ? I mean, I can't be . . . it's not possible . . ."

"Here," said Lucien, reaching forward and sliding the book on the table toward him. Trey turned it over in his hands and read the faded lettering of the title: *The Book of Werewolves* by Sabine Baring-Gould.

"That should tell you almost everything you need to know about your 'condition.' There are also other books here in the library for you to explore, should you wish, but none are as comprehensive as that tome. It is not a reference book, Trey, but it should give you some background history about your kind. You will have questions. Lots and lots of questions. Ask anything you want, and Alexa and I will try to answer."

Trey was numb. He realized how preposterous he must look, sitting there with his staring eyes and his mouth open. He tried to identify the emotion that filled him right now, struggling at first, until he realized that he had experienced it before. It was despair. It was the same feeling of soul-crushing despair that he had felt at the death of his grandmother, and now, as then, it seemed to have hollowed him out, leaving him completely numb.

Tom came back into the room. Trey didn't look up until the awkward silence that followed had stretched out for some time. The look on the Irishman's face did nothing to alleviate the utter dismay he was feeling. "I just had a call. You might want to come and see what's on the news," he said. And then, under his breath, added in a whisper, "Then again, you might not."

7

Lucien stopped as they entered the living room, turning to look at the television that was on and tuned in to one of the twenty-four-hour news channels. Text scrolled along the bottom of the screen and a sign in the top left-hand corner announced that they were witnessing "Breaking News."

"Police are still trying to ascertain exactly how many people were in the building at the time of the fire . . ." The reporter, holding a microphone bearing the name of his news channel, was standing in front of a cordoned-off area of police tape. Behind him a fire engine had pulled up—firefighters disembarked and instantly assumed the roles that they had practiced a thousand times. Trey watched as a number of men in full safety equipment struggled against the power of the hose they were using to spray a thick, foaming substance into the heart of the flames. The reporter facing the camera had his collar up and shoulders hunched to shelter himself from the intense heat at his back.

". . . firefighters have been struggling for over an hour now to bring the situation under control," the reporter continued. "An insider within the force has told us that at this stage they cannot rule out foul play."

Trey watched as a police officer ushered back a small crowd of people braving the cold night air to gawk at the conflagration. As the crowd moved back he caught a glimpse of a little lime-green car parked in one of the spaces behind the fire engine.

Wendy had bought the car from her mum when she had first got the job at the care home. She'd proudly driven it in on her third day, parking it in a spot just down from the one it was in now. The children had teased her about the car's color, calling it the Kermitmobile, but Wendy had just laughed along with them, telling them that it was her pride and joy. She even had a name for it, Trey remembered: Priscilla.

". . . early reports suggest that there were twelve children and five staff members at the home. It is not yet known how many, if any, managed to escape the blaze. This is Giles Fox, outside the Apple Grove Care Home, for Sky News."

The picture cut back to the studio, where the anchorman introduced an expert on fire prevention. But for Trey the world had stopped turning. He was oblivious to everything around him, the picture of those flames licking at the sky from the roof of the building playing over and over in his mind.

He'd hated the care home. He'd hated the fact that he had to live there in its sterile, loveless atmosphere while other children lucky enough not to be abandoned or orphaned lived in *proper* homes. But seeing it in flames like that, hearing the news of the carnage that the fire appeared to have caused, made him feel . . . lost. Utterly lost. There was nothing now. There was no one and no thing that he could identify with or cling to for support, and he felt more alone than he had since his grandmother had died. He put his head in his hands and tried to hold back the blackness that built up inside him.

A huge, rending pain tore through his stomach and spread—like the fire on the screen that had ripped through that building—into every cell in his body. A high, keening screech escaped him and he sank to his knees, tearing at skin that felt as if a thousand rusted nails were bursting through its surface.

"Quick!" shouted Lucien. "He is going to transform, we need to get him somewhere safe."

Lucien and Tom moved swiftly to the boy's side to see if they might be able to get him to his feet, but Trey was writhing on the floor, his arms and legs lashing out in all directions.

Without thinking of the danger, Lucien bent over and picked the boy up as though he were a child's toy, ignoring the deluge of kicks and punches that landed upon his face and body, one opening up a large gash under his left eye.

He placed Trey carefully onto one of the chairs and turned to look at his daughter. "He needs help, Alexa. He is not ready, not yet anyway, and to change into a werewolf now, under these circumstances, could be disastrous—he's simply too volatile. Please, try to help him."

Trey's face was a pinched mask of agony. It had taken on a livid red hue, and a film of sweat covered every inch of him as he bucked and writhed in the chair. They could feel the heat pouring off him, and Tom exchanged a worried look with Lucien as he stood helplessly by the boy's side.

As they watched, Trey's lips peeled back and he sucked in a ragged breath through clenched teeth. His hands—fingers rigidly set into hooks as if he were grasping an invisible tennis ball—were the same angry red color as his face, and, as they watched, the tips of black claws like the ends of a crab's hooked pincers started to erupt from the flesh of his fingertips. A multitude of coarse hairs appeared to push through his skin from invisible pores.

Trey screamed again and threw himself against the back of the chair, the wooden supports behind the padding cracking and splintering under the force of the attack. His fists were now balled tightly, and small droplets of blood escaped them as the emerging talons bit deep into the fleshy palms beneath.

Alexa knelt down in front of him, her hands pressing down on his legs in an attempt to hold them still.

"Trey . . . Trey, listen to me; it's Alexa."

Trey could hear her calm voice speaking directly into his mind and a silvery-pink wedge of color cut through the black swirling pain. That gentle but persistent nudging feeling in his brain was back again.

"You need to take control, Trey. You are stronger than the forces that are flooding through you now, and you can

make this stop. But you must take control. If you become the werewolf now, with the anger and pain that you are feeling—heaven knows what the consequences might be. You could kill us all. Please, Trey, fight it and take control."

Lucien and Tom could only look on as the boy's body continued to spasm in agony. His face was beginning to distort, the flesh around his nose and mouth becoming tight and waxy as it started to distend outward.

Another strangled scream escaped him and his lips curled back over his teeth, which were thickening and extending out of his gums.

"Trey, breathe deeply and try to follow my voice out of the blackness. Breathe, Trey. That's it, follow my voice . . ."

The silvery-pink color was more vibrant now, and was interspersed with golds and oranges. The colors that he began to associate with Alexa's voice seemed to push against the angry blacks and reds that had filled his head, and the pain started to abate, his jerking body slowly relaxing until finally he was still.

Alexa stood up and watched Trey as he sank back into the wrecked chair, trying to control his breathing, which came and went in a series of harsh, half-broken judders. Finally he opened his eyes and looked up at them.

Lucien took a small step forward and leaned toward him, puffing out his cheeks. He smiled a sad smile and placed his hand on top of the boy's. "You scared the living daylights out of us for a while there, Trey. But the control that you showed proves to me that you can master the powers that lie within you. Your father would have been very proud of you."

"I'll get that tea," said Tom, hurrying hastily in the direction of the kitchen.

Trey opened his hands and looked at the oozing cuts. They had already stopped bleeding and they seemed to fizz. He lifted a hand closer to him and thought that he could actually make out the edges of the wounds starting to knit together. When he inspected them again an hour later the only evidence that they had ever been damaged was the dried blood that remained smeared across his skin.

"The care home," Trey whispered. "They're all dead, aren't they?"

"Yes, Trey. It would appear that there were no survivors," Lucien answered in a quiet voice. "I'm truly sorry."

"And it was me that they were after, wasn't it?"

"I'm afraid so. The other adults and children would have been considered nothing more than collateral damage, but it was you that they would have wanted dead, and fire is one of the methods that are actually effective in dispatching one of your kind."

A sad smile flashed across Trey's face, quickly disappearing as soon as it had appeared.

"One of my kind," he repeated.

He looked up at Lucien, who was still looking down at him with genuine concern. "Do you know who did this, Lucien?"

"Yes, I do. But I think it best that you rest now and—"

"No. I want to know who is responsible for this. I want to know who could do such a thing."

"Please trust me. You need to rest. Tomorrow I will tell you absolutely everything that I know. But you must rest now." Lucien held out a hand to Trey and, when the boy took it, helped him gently to his feet.

Trey stood and held up his hand to wave away any further help. He swallowed and fought back the tears that threatened to take him over. "OK. I'll do as you say." He stood facing him, a determined look on his face. "Before I do, though, I want you at least to tell me his name. Then tomorrow you can tell me all that you know."

Lucien nodded and met the boy's eyes. "He's an extraordinarily powerful vampire who is responsible for much pain and suffering in this world. His name is Caliban." He paused, looking at Trey in a way that the teenager found particularly uncomfortable, before adding, "He's my brother."

8

Trey lay on his bed and flicked through the book that Lucien had given him the night before, glancing again at the ancient drawings and depictions of werewolves. Much of the book was taken up with legend and folklore regarding werewolves throughout the world, and he tossed it aside again—as he had done on countless occasions throughout the night and early morning. He hadn't slept much more than an hour or so all night, and when he did close his eyes, terrible visions of his friends screaming in their burning beds filled the void behind his eyelids. Once, during the early hours of the morning, he'd got up to vomit as the nightmarish scenes looped over and over in his imagination.

Nothing was normal anymore. All his life he had dreamed of adventure. He'd wanted nothing more than to escape and seek out a new life that was not full of stupid house rules and obsequious kids who thought that obedience would win them a family that loved them and cared for them.

Be careful what you wish for, he thought, and smiled sadly up at the ceiling.

He felt empty. Completely and utterly alone in a way that he had never thought was possible. He had always kept pretty much to himself in the care home and school. He'd come to accept this, gradually coming to terms with a life of solitude and loneliness. But now he felt different. It was as though fate, not content with taking his parents and grandmother away from him, wanted him to know that he would always be truly alone. Hell, it turned out that *he wasn't even human*, and now to be told that he was the last of his kind was the final straw.

He reached for the book again but abandoned the idea, taking instead a sheet of paper from the bedside table that he had placed there earlier. In an effort to try to exorcise the visions of the fire, he had set about making notes from the book, trying to clarify the things that he had found out about werewolves, and producing a list of questions that he wanted to ask Lucien and Alexa. He looked at his handwritten notes.

Lyco Facts:
Three ways of becoming werewolf: One/ both parents are lycos (the second is very rare due to only female werewolves being bite survivors), survive an attack by a werewolf (also rare), or through use of sorcery. (Is this true?)

Virtually impossible for humans to kill. Most wounds from "normal" weapons will hurt but not kill. Usual methods of killing a lycanthrope include: beheading, burning in a fire, drowning, and destroying the body so utterly (e.g., with explosives) that they are unable to rejuvenate as they would from most wounds.

All werewolves are ruled by the full moon, but some older,

experienced werewolves have been known to be able to change at other times.

　　Werewolves are nether-creatures (?). As such they belong to the Netherworld—*what is this?*

Werewolf Myths:
Silver bullets/ daggers/ arrows/ swords only means of destroying a lyco. Index and middle finger are same length. Prone to epilepsy. Love of rare meat. Redheaded. Will change back to human if iron or steel thrown over head. (*All complete rubbish*)

Questions:
Netherworld
Amulet and full moon
What happened to the other werewolves? Am I really the last?
Theiss legend—what is this all about?

N.B. Ask Lucien for a book about *vampires*.

　　He sighed, swung his legs off the bed, and looked at the clock on the bedside table. It was four o'clock in the morning.

　　He was about to get up and have a shower—possibly go into the living room and tune in for the latest news—when there was the quietest of knocks upon his door.

　　He paused for a second, not sure that he had actually heard the sound, but sensing someone outside his room, he quietly answered.

"Come in."

Lucien opened the door and entered. He was dressed in gray flannel trousers and a black V-neck sweater. He carried a steaming mug in his hand.

"My, what keen ears you have, Grandma," he said, with a little smile. "I've brought you some tea. I was sure that you would be awake, but didn't know whether you wanted to be alone."

"No, it's fine. I need to talk to someone, Lucien, and it would appear that my options in that department are somewhat limited and diminishing rapidly."

He looked at the vampire standing in his doorway holding the cup in his hands. He wanted to beg him to stop all this, to turn it all back and give him his boring little life again. He wanted to blame him for everything that had happened, but a part of him knew that it was not Lucien's fault—in fact, it occurred to him that this tea-drinking vampire was now his only hope of ever knowing how to live anything approaching a normal life.

Lucien held his look and nodded sadly as if reading the boy's thoughts. He placed the cup on the chest of drawers by the door and pushed the door open wider with his foot.

"Please come with me, Trey. You might want to put your bathrobe on." Lucien held the door open for him and motioned Trey toward the kitchen. Once inside, he slid back one of the giant windows and stepped out onto a balcony that hung outside the building.

The two of them leaned against the balcony's metal

railing and looked down at the river Thames below. The moon was still out, and its quicksilver reflection danced back at them from the broken waves of the great river like a thousand shattered mirrors. The city was slumbering, and while a huge metropolis like London never truly sleeps, very few things moved around in the streets on either side of the waterway's banks.

"Lucien," Trey said, finally breaking the silence, "why does Caliban want me dead?"

The vampire paused, considering his answer before replying.

"Fear, I suppose. If it is possible for a creature like Caliban to feel fear. You see, there are very few things that can actually take on a vampire, Trey, and you are the last in a bloodline of those who have done, and done so successfully. That is why he has dedicated so much effort to eradicating your kind. You were a rare breed before, but he has hunted down and killed almost all of the true-blood werewolves." He turned his eyes on the boy and it seemed to Trey that for a moment they blazed with some unseen light. "Almost . . . but not quite all."

"But—"

"Did you read the section in the book about Theiss?"

"The part that somebody has underlined? Yes."

"'Both I and my brothers are the Hounds of God,'" Lucien said, quoting the passage as he stared out at the river again. "'We are the warriors who go to do battle with demons, and through our efforts we will ensure that the Devil and his minions will not carry off the abundance of the earth down to the Netherworld.' Those were the words that he said to the court as he stood accused of witchcraft." He turned to look back at Trey. "They burned him at the stake."

"I'm sorry, Lucien, what has this got to do with—"

"The legend that surrounds Theiss is one that you may or may not choose to believe. He foresaw that a nether-creature would rise to such power in the Netherworld that it would be capable of launching a series of attacks on humankind to eventually bring it to its knees, leaving the humans as little more than cattle for the forces of the Netherworld to feed upon at will. Theiss also said that it would be a werewolf—a true-blood werewolf—that would stop this nether-creature. My brother believes the legend. Moreover, he believes that he is the creature in the legend, and that you are the werewolf in his way."

Even above the wind, Trey could hear the roaring sound of his blood as it sped through his body. "I'm just a kid," he said.

"So you keep saying. And I keep telling you that you are no longer 'just a kid.' You have a great power within you, and it is up to you to realize that."

A silence followed as Trey tried to take in what he had just been told. If it was true, he was at real risk of losing his life to some psychopathic bloodsucker because of a legend that some madman had contrived hundreds of years ago.

"How did my parents really die?" Trey asked.

If Lucien was surprised by the change of subject, he

90

didn't show it. "They were murdered." He turned his face to the wind, blinking as it licked around his features. "Your father and I went on a mission together: We had become alerted that a particularly nasty djinn had escaped from the Netherworld into the human plane. The demon was too powerful for me to stop alone, and despite my promise not to call upon him, I asked for your father's help." The vampire stopped and stared down at a point in the river below. "Caliban murdered your mother while your father and I were away. When he found out what had happened, your father set out to hunt Caliban down and avenge your mother's death. Finally, after three months, he located him on an island in Tahiti and tried to raise a force against him. He did this without me because he knew that I would have tried to slow him down, tried to make him more cautious."

He paused and tapped one of the fingernails of his manicured hands against the hollow aluminium rods that made up the guardrail. "Your father picked the wrong people to go into alliance with, and before he could attack my brother, his so-called allies were bought off and turned against him." Looking up at Trey, he seemed to be weighing up how much he could reveal in one go, gauging the boy's fragility before continuing.

"He was beheaded and his body was burned in a fire pit on the island of Moorea. As soon as I found out where he was and what he was planning, I went out there to stop him. But it was too late: He was already dead and my brother was gone."

"Why my mother? What had she done?"

Lucien shook his head. "She gave birth to you."

Trey took this in as he looked out across the sickly metal halide-lit streets of Docklands. A cold wind tugged at the hem of his bathrobe.

He didn't feel a world-shattering shock at learning the true story about the deaths of his parents, though he had always believed them to have been killed in a car accident. There was just a great, vast, black, empty void inside him now that nothing seemed to permeate.

Trey stared over at the creature standing next to him. He couldn't look at Lucien without thinking of what he really was: an undead, blood-craving abomination. And yet, this thing had shown him nothing but kindness and respect since they had met.

He felt unable to cope with the sheer enormity of the revelations that had been made to him. He was aware, however, that something in his makeup had changed and that there was no going back to the way he was before.

Lucien looked over at him as if sensing the apprehension and fear that he was experiencing. "I know," he said, nodding his head sadly, reaching over to pat the boy on the forearm.

"No, you don't," Trey replied.

He looked at Lucien's hand as it rested on the handrail beside him. He frowned at the smoothness of the skin on the back of the hand and the neatly manicured nails at the end of the slender fingers.

92

"Vampires don't shape-shift, do they, Lucien? Not in the way that you described to me yesterday, I mean," Trey asked.

Lucien looked over at him again, small creases momentarily forming in the gap between his eyebrows. "No," he said, "we can *mist*—which to anyone else would look like we were teleporting. In this way, we are able to disappear and reappear a short distance away almost instantaneously. But we are always in our vampire form. The bats are, unfortunately, a Hollywood invention. Why?" he asked, with a puzzled smile.

"I just assumed that vampires would all have the stereotypical fangs and claws that we see and read about. I mean, I would have thought those things were quite useful to a bloodsucking creature of the night." Trey regretted the venom in his tone. Lucien had done nothing to deserve his anger, but something in him wanted to make the older man feel uncomfortable.

"I had them removed some time ago. Yes, before you ask, I still require a daily consumption of human blood. But, among my other businesses, I happen to own a blood research laboratory outside Oxford and so have a constant safe supply. Alexa, on the other hand, as a halfling, can suffice with a simple daily injection of a hemoglobin derivative, which she self-administers using an EpiPen. Besides," he continued, "my fangs reminded me of a time that I would rather try to forget, when I was younger and followed the desires that my kind are reviled for. I did some terrible things when I was younger, Trey, and now I must atone for those things. The work I do—that your father did—is my attempt to put some of those horrors right."

"Those people at the home—some of them were good people," Trey said, looking down at his feet. "People like Wendy and . . . they died because of me, didn't they?"

"It wasn't your fault. You must never think that," Lucien said. "If you had been there instead of here with us, you too would be among the ashes of your dead friends. If you truly want to honor your friends and family, join us in helping to stop my brother and his forces."

Trey shivered as the cold wind blowing off the river ghosted through the balcony, bringing with it the sharp metallic smell of the water's surface.

"What happened to me last night, Lucien? Why did I start to change?"

"The strong emotions you were experiencing caused you to start transforming into the werewolf. That can, and will, happen, very rarely, during moments of extreme duress, but as you discovered last night, you have the power within you to suppress and control it. I have to say that it is impressive for one as young as you to have mastered such control at such an early stage of your lycanthropy."

Trey paused, remembering, before going on. "The pain—it was intolerable. It felt as though my skin was being torn off. Every cell of my body was on fire and it consumed me.

I don't think that I could take that pain again and again, Lucien. Death would be a better option than that."

Lucien looked at him and nodded his head in understanding. He reached forward and hooked the silver chain that hung inside Trey's pajama top with his thumb. Gently he pulled it toward him, until it stretched taut against the back of Trey's neck, the silver amulet jittering against the chain in front of him.

"The pain will not be like that when you *choose* to transform, Trey." Lucien released the chain, and clasped his hand on Trey's shoulder, giving him a gentle reassuring shake. "This amulet will help, but you must master your condition, and when you have, you will change from man to werewolf in an instant." He clicked his finger next to Trey's ear. "Just like that."

He stepped back and slid open the window behind him. "We will begin your training this afternoon. I want you to transform voluntarily, and we will all get a chance to see what you are made of. I, for one, am intrigued to see the wolf that lies inside you, Trey. And we must prepare you for what lies ahead. We will talk again shortly. There are still many things about Caliban and the dangers that lie ahead that you must know."

He turned from the balcony and disappeared inside.

Trey turned back to the river, pulling his bathrobe around him against the cold wind that blew in off the waterway's surface. A squat tugboat cut through the choppy waters below, churning up a dirty gray wake as it forged its way through the black surface. Trey watched it battle its way against the tide before disappearing around the bend far away to his left.

I, for one, am intrigued to see the wolf that lies inside you.

He shuddered.

Stranger in a Strange Land, he thought. The title of a book that he'd read a few months before came into his head. He wondered why this story should suddenly come back to him and then smiled ruefully at himself, remembering the ending of the book and how the lead character was brutally killed. He hoped it wasn't a portent.

"We're a long way from Kansas, Toto," he said to himself, and turned to follow Lucien back inside.

9

Trey returned to his room and stayed there for the rest of the morning. He was hiding and he knew it, but he needed to get away from these people and his room seemed to be the only place left to him. He'd showered, standing under the hot needles of water for almost an hour, playing the events of the last twenty-four hours over and over in his mind and coming up with the same questions and conclusions. Eventually he dressed, and lay on his bed, staring up at the ceiling.

At eleven o'clock there was a knock on his door. "Come in," Trey said.

He was surprised when he saw that it was Tom who opened the door. The tall Irishman stood in the opening as if he was loath to cross the divide that separated Trey and his solitude from the rest of the house. "Y'all right?" he eventually asked.

"Yeah, I suppose," Trey answered.

"The others have gone out. Alexa has gone shopping with her friend Stephanie, and Lucien's setting everything up downstairs for your little session this afternoon." He looked over at the boy, weighing him up. "Do you fancy a bite to eat and a cup of tea? Mrs. Magilton's just left, but she's made up a ton of sandwiches for you and me. It'd be a shame to waste them." He paused, stepping away from the door, but leaving it open and not retreating fully. "Besides, you and I haven't had a chance to have a chat yet."

Trey slowly swung his legs over the side of the bed and sat up, looking over at the Irishman. "What kind of sandwiches?" he asked eventually.

"You name it, she's made it. C'mon, you've got another big day ahead of you, and as my old ma used to say, 'You can't stand up an empty sack.'" He turned his back on Trey then and walked off in the direction of the kitchen.

Trey followed Tom and sat down at one of the chairs. The kettle was already making scratchy sounds as its element began to heat up, and Tom was retrieving a couple of mugs from the cupboard over the sink.

The morning papers were still on the table, their headlines full of stories about the fire at the care home. Trey pushed them aside, not wishing to see the grisly pictures inked on the covers.

Trey looked over at the broad back of the Irishman as he prepared the tea. "How long have you worked for him?" Trey asked, cocking his head at Tom. It was a question that had been nagging at him (along with the other one that he hadn't asked: "How can you bear to work for him?").

"Jeez, I don't rightly know. Longer than I care to remember." Tom placed a tea towel on the counter and leaned over to look down at Trey from the raised kitchen area. "You can trust him, Trey. I know this whole thing is like you've fallen down the rabbit hole and are suddenly trapped in some drug-fueled Lewis Carroll nightmare, but you can trust him. He's only got your best interests at heart."

He went back to making the tea, leaving Trey to think about this.

"Did he ask you to have a chat with me, Tom?"

"Lord, no. Something like that wouldn't occur to Lucien. He's worried, all right—worried that you'll simply walk away and try to work this through yourself—but I think he believes that you'll come round eventually, you know, once you've come to terms with everything. By the way, I wouldn't really recommend the walking-away thing; this world has changed for you, and you're going to need all the help you can get to cope . . . and survive."

For some reason Trey had the distinct feeling that this was the most that Tom had spoken to anyone in a long time, and wondered if this stern individual was simply glad to have somebody *normal* around the place. Despite his harsh looks and gruff manner, there was something about Tom that made Trey feel at ease in his company. Maybe it was because Tom didn't seem to expect anything from him—he seemed to understand the confusion that Trey was feeling better than Alexa or Lucien. Or maybe it was because the man seemed so self-assured and some of that simply rubbed off on the people around him.

"I just don't feel comfortable in his company," Trey said after a while. "I can't look at him without thinking about what he is and what he might have done."

Tom brought the tea around and set one of the mugs in front of Trey. He leaned over and unwrapped the Saran wrap from around the mountain of sandwiches set in the middle of the table, picking one of the dainty little triangles up in his big shovel hands and putting it whole into his mouth. "Are you scared of him?" he asked.

"Of course I am," Trey admitted, "but it's weird, you know; it's more than just fear. Every time I'm near Lucien I feel this great tide of anger building up inside of me. I'm not like that, Tom; I'm not an angry person."

Tom pointed to the food and nodded his encouragement to Trey to join him in eating. He chewed thoughtfully on another sandwich, and Trey felt no need to break the silence that filled the room.

"It's only natural that you should feel angry with Lucien. Jeez, he practically abducts you from that care home, tells you that he's a vampire, tells *you* that you've become a werewolf, drops the bombshell that his own brother is the murderer of your parents and that that same brother is hell-bent on wiping you off the face of the earth as well. It's hardly a surprise that the harbinger of doom isn't exactly top of your Christmas card list."

Trey nodded and picked up one of the sandwiches. "How did you come to work for him?" he asked.

Tom set down his mug and put his finger in his mouth, picking at a piece of food that had become lodged in one of his teeth.

"When I was a young man living in Ireland, I was a bit

100

of a hell-raiser. You know the type—the kind of cocky young fellow that thinks they're bulletproof. A tough nut. Not a nice person to be around." He picked up another sandwich and looked down at its surface. "I fell in with a bad crowd. And some of these people . . . well, they weren't quite what they seemed." He chewed on the food that he had managed to dislodge, and stared out of the window for a moment, remembering.

"One weekend we'd planned to have a party at my uncle's farm. He was going away on holiday, so we had the run of the place to ourselves. I was supposed to go over there on Saturday morning to get the place sorted, get the drinks and food in. But I finished work early on Friday and decided to go to the farm then instead. I was on my way through to the farmhouse with the groceries that I'd picked up when I heard a noise in the barn. Thinking that it was kids messing about, I decided to investigate. What I witnessed that night changed my life forever."

He looked at Trey, and his eyes were hard to meet. "Unbeknown to any of the rest of us, two members of our little gang were vampires. They'd abducted a young lass who had been out on her bachelorette party in the local village. When I walked in, they were in the process of tearing the poor thing apart, draining her of the blood and life that flowed through her body. When I tried to stop them, they set upon me, beating me to within an inch of my life. I believed that they were going to finish feasting on the girl and then start in on me. They beat me mercilessly until I lost consciousness.

That's how I ended up with this pretty little memento." He fingered the ugly disfigurement on his right cheek.

"And that, as they say, would have been the end of me. But just as I was slipping away, a man walked in. When I came to, the two vampires were dead and the man was trying to save the girl's life. He was too late to save her, but he managed to get me out of there in one piece and patch me up again. Lucien saved my life—in more ways than one, I think—and I have been with him ever since."

A silence filled the kitchen, punctuated by Tom taking a noisy slurp from his mug.

"Thanks, Tom," Trey said.

"What for?"

"For telling me all of that. Thanks."

Tom nodded his head. He frowned over at Trey and nodded again toward the sandwiches. "Are you going to eat these things or let them all go stale? You're going to need every ounce of energy for this afternoon."

"What's Lucien planning for me?" Trey asked, biting into a cheese-and-tomato sandwich.

Tom grinned, a wicked light dancing in those flinty eyes of his. "You'll see soon enough," he said.

10

Alexa arrived back at the apartment just after noon, bustling through the doors with assorted shopping bags, the names of famous department stores adorning their multicolored exteriors. She dropped them in a heap by the side of the settee and threw herself backward into the soft leather cushions, letting out a big, weary sigh in the process.

Tom, who was sitting in one of the easy chairs reading a paper, looked over the top of his silver-rimmed spectacles at her, small creases radiating from the corners of his eyes as he surveyed the jumble of bags. "Just a *small* shopping expedition today, Alexa? What happened? Have you maxed out your card again?"

"No, Tom," Alexa replied wearily. "I had to get back, remember? Dad told me that I was to give Trey a quick tour of the place before they get started this afternoon. Where is he?" she asked.

"I'm here," Trey said, walking in. He looked down at the bags at the end of the settee, whistling through his teeth. "Blimey!" he said. "How many people have you been shopping for?"

"Don't you start," Alexa said, sitting up. "I get enough

grief from Tom here; I expected a little more support from someone nearer my own age. Anyway, I bought you this," she said, sliding over to reach into one of the bags. She held up a pink-and-gray sweater that Trey would not have been seen dead in. "What do you think? It's cashmere and it's Paul Smith."

Trey caught sight of Tom pushing his glasses up the bridge of his nose and burying his head in his paper.

"Er, well . . . yeah. It's nice of you and everything, Alexa, but I don't think it's really my thing. It's a bit . . . stripy." Trey held contact with her eyes so that he wouldn't have to look at Tom, who was shifting around in his seat trying to stifle a laugh.

She smiled caustically at the Irishman, standing up to face Trey. "Are you ready?" she asked.

"What for?" Trey replied.

"The grand tour—not that it's much of a tour or very grand, but Dad wants you to see the place so that you know what's what."

"Oh. Then lead on, Macduff," Trey said.

Alexa looked at him quizzically.

"My grandma always used to say that whenever we went anywhere. I never realized it was a misquote until we read *Macbeth* in English last year. I think I like my gran's version better, though."

"Come on, then. Let's get this over with as painlessly as possible."

She moved to the elevator, the doors opening instantly

104

as she pressed the button to call the elevator. They entered, Trey standing beside her and breathing in her perfume as she depressed the button to descend to the first floor. He'd got the impression that he had hurt her feelings with his comment about the sweater, and the silence that filled the elevator as they descended seemed to reinforce this notion.

The doors of the elevator opened up to reveal a bustling office scene. The tickety-tap sound of people typing into computer keyboards and the ringing of telephones punctuated the general hubbub of the room.

Trey and Alexa stepped out of the lift. "This is one of my father's businesses and it takes up the entire first floor," Alexa said, as she led Trey through the rows of low booths that separated the office workers from each other.

"I don't pretend to know who most of these people are, or what they do, but this place is all about information gathering. The staff is split about seventy–thirty between nether-creatures and humans, the majority being demons of one sort or another. Tom is the overall manager and I'm sure that he'd be more than willing to avail you of all the intricate details, if you're interested." She started to move forward again, but Trey hooked her arm by the elbow to stop her.

"Hang on a minute. Did you say most of the people here are demons?" Trey looked at the office scene in front of him, deep creases forming on his forehead as he looked at the workers going about their tasks. It all looked perfectly *normal* to him.

"That's right. It makes sense really. Our employees investigate and stop the more nefarious goings-on that involve nether-creatures in the human realm. What's the saying? It takes a thief to catch a thief?"

"Stop just a minute, Alexa," Trey said, pulling her back again. "The Netherworld and the earth . . . they coexist, right? Like parallel worlds?"

"Yes, something like that."

"And you are telling me that demons and other . . . nether-creatures can cross from their world into ours?"

"And vice versa. There are portals between the worlds that have existed since time began. In addition, temporary portals can be summoned by anyone powerful and knowledgeable enough in magic to create one."

"And you're telling me that there are *demons* here now?" Trey looked around again and shook his head slowly. "But everyone looks normal," he said in a quiet voice.

Alexa followed the line that his sight took, a frown forming on her forehead. When she looked at Trey again, her mouth was hanging open and she had turned a subtle shade of pink. "I completely forgot: You can't see them, can you? Oh, Trey, I am so sorry; that was bloody stupid of me. You see, they use a masking spell to hide their true appearance, a sort of human shell that provides them perfect camouflage in this world. Other nether-creatures can see *through* this shell. It's hard to explain—it's like you're looking at someone through a transparent mannequin, you can see the mannequin moving and talking at the same time as the real creature inside, but you know that it isn't the real thing.

"The good news," she continued, "is that when you morph into a werewolf, you'll be able to see them, but in your human form, you're unable to see their true demon form."

"But you can see them. You told me that you weren't a nether-creature."

"It's a spell. It's difficult to learn, but it enables humans to see through the demon disguise. It took Tom almost a year to learn." She grinned at him. "But then again, he hates magic."

Trey shook his head and stared about him again.

"One of the tech-bods who works at one of my father's other companies invented a headset that allowed anyone to see things as if they were being viewed by a nether-creature, but it was a great unwieldy thing and they decided to scrap the idea."

"Hello, Alexa!" A cheery-looking woman waved from her desk as they passed.

"Hi, Ruth. Oh, thanks for those manuscripts that you copied for me last week—they were incredibly interesting," she said, waving back. "Ruth is a darling and can help locate almost anything that you might need to know about polter-geists and telekinesis. It's her *thing*," she confided in Trey.

"Is *she* a demon?" asked Trey in a low whisper, looking back at the plump woman in the summer dress who was busily tapping at her keyboard again.

Alexa made a face. "No, Ruth's a human. She gets

messages from the dead that turn up on little notes in her handbag, though. Neat, huh?"

She walked away from him, stopping in front of one of two wooden doors at the end of the office. She opened the door and walked inside, beckoning him to follow her. "This is the research library." She closed the door behind them to reveal a large room with a horseshoe of tables in the center of its dimly lit interior. Arranged around the inside of the tables' curve were a number of freestanding lamps. The light from a couple of these was being used by two people hunched over a jumble of books and maps laid out in front of them. They briefly glanced up before returning to their studies.

"My father owns the entire building," Alexa went on in a quiet voice. "It used to be a grain warehouse, but he had it converted about twenty-five years ago.

"This is a good place to start to find answers to some of the questions that you'll have tumbling around in that head of yours at the moment."

She walked across the room toward a strange-looking machine built into the wall on their right. It looked like an enormous fridge without doors, and Trey reckoned that it was at least four meters wide and as tall as he was. Alexa pressed a button, and a sickly blue light blinked on inside the device. Trey saw that it was some kind of automated storage system (of the kind that you see in a pharmacist's shop), and as Alexa punched a number into the keypad, the columns of shelves started to move, shifting down into the bowels of the machinery to be replaced by others from above.

Each shelf held up to about twenty books that were all carefully laid out on their backs, and Trey could see, as row after row came into sight before disappearing again, that some of them were incredibly old—barely books at all, but sheaths of puckered parchment bound together by tattered and beaten materials impossible to define.

"Here," she said, holding out a dog-eared volume that she had retrieved from one of the shelves. "A bit more background reading for you."

"What is it?"

"It's a book on vampires. Probably the most comprehensive book ever written on them. It tells you about their physiology, their history, how they survive, and how to . . ."

"How to kill them?" Trey said, staring at her.

"Yes, that's included too. I thought you might be interested."

Trey shook his head angrily. "It's not true, you know."

"What isn't?"

"The legend. Lucien told me the story of Theiss and his visions. It isn't true. I'm not looking to fulfill some crazy prophecy that was made by some guy as he was roasting on the stake."

"I know. But it can't harm, knowing what kind of creature you are going to be living with, can it? Neither can it hurt to know what type of creature it is that wants to kill you."

She nodded at the book in his hand before turning around to switch off the machine.

"Where does all the money come from?" Trey asked. He gestured with his chin at the office outside. "How does your father make his money?"

"Like I said, I don't pretend to understand most of what goes on. But my father provides security for other global corporations. Some years ago, Caliban realized that he could undermine humanity by attacking big business. If he could infiltrate all the big financial institutions, the electronics companies, the energy companies, the arms manufacturers— the list goes on—he could wield great power in this world. My father's people try to balk him in these enterprises. In addition, my father uses certain *skills* possessed by various demons to help companies find the things that they want: oil, gas, diamonds, gold. People are willing to pay *very* handsomely for those skills."

They left, closing the door behind them. "The other room is much the same, but it's stacked out with computer equipment. That's where I do most of my homework," Alexa said.

"You still go to school?" Trey asked, following in her wake as they walked back through the busy office. "I thought that you might not bother, or that you'd have private tutors."

She stopped to press the button for the lift, the doors sliding open immediately. "No, Trey, I go to school. I like the normality that it provides me," she said as he stepped in beside her. "Dad will probably insist that you go too.

110

"The top floor, as you know, is our apartment and you can explore any areas of that you haven't seen yet on your own—there are no out-of-bounds, except my bedroom. Oh, and if you value the current location of your testicles, I wouldn't go snooping around in Tom's room without permission either." She smiled as the elevator bell pinged and the doors slid open to reveal the second floor.

They stepped out into a long narrow corridor with three doors leading off on each side.

"This is the gym," she said, opening the first door on the right to reveal a fully equipped aerobic suite complete with running, rowing, and cross-training machines of various types. The far wall was dedicated to free weights. A pressing bench and a squat stand sat between shelves lined with dumbbells and metal discs. "There's a boxing ring with bags and stuff through that door over there."

She closed the door and opened an identical-looking one on the other side of the corridor. "This is a dance studio," she said, revealing a wooden-floored expanse with a mirrored wall and ballet bar at one end. "If you want a personal trainer, I'm sure that we can set one up for you. Or you can join Tom or my father in their workouts if you'd prefer."

They continued up the corridor. Alexa pointed to the doors set across from each other at the far end. "The two farthest doors are his and hers changing rooms with showers and toilets—they both lead through to another elevator that takes you to the pool up on the roof."

Moving up to the two central doors, she gestured over

her shoulder at the door to her rear. "Sauna and steam rooms are in there, but today," she said, pushing open the last of the doors, "we are in here."

They walked through into a dim area that had a series of tiered seats arranged on either side of a short gangway. Directly in front were two glass-backed squash courts, and Trey noticed that the central wall separating the two courts was missing, doubling the floor space. He peered into the courts, trying to locate where the wall could have gone to, but seeing no obvious signs, assumed that it must be retractable, like the giant television upstairs.

The bright lights of the squash courts were on, the harsh illumination spilling out into the darkened observation area. In one corner of the court was a pile of what appeared to be thick gymnastic mats and tackle pads of the sort that you might use in rugby training. Apart from that, the courts were empty.

"Ah, there you are," shouted Lucien from somewhere over Trey's left shoulder. He turned to look up and could see Tom, Lucien, and another man sitting high up in the raked seating toward the back of the room. As they stood and moved down toward them, Trey noticed that Lucien was wearing a tracksuit and couldn't help but think how peculiar it looked on him.

"This is Hopper." Lucien introduced the stranger to Trey, who shook his hand. "He'll be helping out with our little session this afternoon."

"Nice to meet you, young man. A real, honest-to-God

112

lycanthrope, eh? Has he told you you're the last one? Yes? Well, not exactly the last werewolf, but the last *natural*. You're unique, you know, yes, unique. It's an honor to shake your hand, it is." Hopper never kept still the whole time he was talking. There was something unnerving about the way he kept nodding at Trey, his piggy little eyes blinking repeatedly as if they had an irritating dust in them that he was trying to blink out. Trey had no idea why, but he took an instant dislike to the little man.

"Never met a natural before," he continued. "Met loads of those bloody idiots that wander around drinking from the footprints of wolves and uttering ancient incantations; they all go bleedin' nuts eventually and end up killing a boatload of people. But never a natural—no, never. In case you were wondering, I'm a sputum djinn."

"Oh, for the love of God," Tom said, turning away in desperation.

"A what?" Trey asked.

"Green, ain't he, this one? Green as the hills of Nongroth," Hopper said, the blink rate cranking up to an alarming level. "A sputum djinn. Technically, the proper nomenclature would have me described as a level-two Orn djinn with spitting attack/defense capabilities. But everyone just refers to us as sputum djinn—more 'catchy,' I suppose. Allow me to demonstrate."

He took a small step back and smiled, revealing two rows of brown, poorly kept teeth. Then he turned to face the transparent wall at the back of the court and spat.

As soon as the discharge left his mouth it seemed to coalesce and grow rapidly into a spherical mass, so that when it hit the wall, where it stuck, there was a football-sized globule of jellylike goo. "There," he said, nodding his head toward it. "Now touch it with your fingers."

"No, thanks," replied Trey, his lip curling in distaste. He couldn't think of anything in the world that he would less like to do.

"Go on," implored the little man. "It's not really *spit* as such. It's just this *stuff* that we sputum djinn are able to produce at will. Go on, it won't hurt." He nudged Trey hard with his elbow toward the wall.

Trey looked at Lucien, who was trying hard not to laugh at the horrified look on the boy's face.

"You might as well," he said, nodding encouragingly. "He won't let up until you do."

Trey gingerly reached out with his fingers and touched the gently quivering ball of gunk.

As soon as his fingers came into contact with the substance, he felt them jerk and sink deeper inside as if the gelatinous goo were grabbing them. Trey flinched and tried to pull his fingers free, but in doing so, his hand seemed to get sucked farther inside until his entire fist was engulfed up to the wrist. As soon as he stopped pulling, the substance seemed to relax slightly in response, but his hand was still trapped.

He looked around anxiously at the four people behind him, who were watching his struggles with amusement.

Hopper was dancing around on the spot and Trey couldn't help but think that he looked like Rumpelstiltskin.

"Let him out now, Hopper," Tom said firmly, noticing the growing distress on Trey's face.

"Can't get out, can you?" Hopper said in a high, excited voice. "Can't escape it, no matter what you do!" He let out a little laugh and pointed to the boy's hand.

"I said let him out, you pus-filled son of a garnog. You've had your fun." Tom pushed Hopper forward toward Trey.

Trey had no idea what a garnog was, but the look on Hopper's face suggested that he was far from pleased at having a parent called one. The demon reached up and placed his hand on Trey's shoulder, and as he did so, Trey's hand simply slid out. It was as if, at the creature's touch, the substance simply ceased to be sticky any longer.

Trey looked down at his fingers and was surprised to see that they were completely dry and that no hint of the substance was evident. He tentatively sniffed them to find that they were also odorless.

Lucien stepped forward. "Hopper is here to provide a little insurance this afternoon should anything start to go wrong. He is incredibly accurate and has sufficient range to render anything . . . or anyone, temporarily immobile within the confines of the space that we will be using. In addition, Tom will be on hand with this rather fearsome-looking weapon." Lucien held up a bizarrely shaped rifle and handed it over to his assistant. From the back it appeared

115

like any other rifle that Trey had seen in movies, with a wooden stock just behind the trigger mechanism. But at the front of the gun—the business end—the barrel diameter was huge, as if someone had pumped it up with a foot pump.

"It's a nonlethal weapon and is used for firing a metal-link net to entrap animals and people. It's quite a new technology, so Hopper is our backup."

Hopper sniffed and looked at the contraption in Tom's hands. "Reckon that that thing's got disaster written all over it. Better off sticking to a tried and trusted method, like old Hopper."

"Be that as it may," Tom retorted, "in this instance, it doesn't pay to be too careful. A man with boots doesn't have to worry about where to put his feet."

"All I'm saying is that we sputum djinn have . . ."

"Will you shut yer bloody piehole, Hopper? Or I'll be going to get a real gun and then we'll see just how fast and accurate you are!"

Trey looked over to Alexa, who was smiling and shaking her head at the bickering that was still going on as the two men stepped through the door at the back of the court. He turned back to Lucien and asked, "So what are we doing?"

"You and I are going in there together," he said, leaning down to pick up a long fiberglass pole from beside the door. He slipped his hand through a leather strap that hung down from one end, allowing the whole thing to dangle from his wrist. Lucien went on. "Then you are going to purposely

116

transform into a werewolf. Then you and I, Mr. Laporte, are going to have a little duel, a sparring session, if you will."

A small laugh escaped Trey's mouth. He looked closely into Lucien's face, his smile fading into a frown.

"You're . . . you're serious, aren't you?"

"Of course," Lucien said, stepping closer to him and continuing. "Trey, I understand that your entire universe has been pulled inside out right now, but you must learn to come to terms with what you are and, more importantly, to harness the powers that you have inherited."

He stepped back a little and surveyed Trey. "Are you going to wear those clothes or did you want to get changed?"

"Do I need to? Or will these do?"

"No, they're fine. I just wondered how much you liked them, that's all."

"Why?"

"Oh, no reason," Lucien replied, and turned to go through the door.

"Are you two coming or what?" shouted Tom from inside, where he had taken up position in one of the corners behind a pile of mats, his gun sticking out from a gap. "Because if you leave me in here much longer with this whinging, phlegm-flinging fool, you'll be picking up little pieces of him for the next few weeks!"

Lucien stopped in the doorway and turned to Trey, one eyebrow raised questioningly.

"Well, are you coming to see just what you are made of, Trey?" he asked.

Trey almost laughed out loud at the absurdity of the situation, but when he looked closely at the vampire standing in front of him, he could see no hint of humor in his eyes. Shaking his head, he followed the vampire through the door to begin his first training session.

11

Lucien stood in front of him, the baton-like implement that he had picked up still hanging from one hand by the wrist strap. He smiled gently at Trey and flicked his eyes about the room, ensuring that everything was in place.

"This will be an experience for both of us, Trey." Lucien's voice rebounded off the concrete walls like the squash balls that they were designed for. Trey thought that he detected a hint of nervousness in it, something that made him feel all the more scared about whatever lay ahead.

"The aim of the exercise is first to get you to fully morph into a werewolf. Your amulet will help ensure that you maintain your human thoughts and intellect while experiencing the full range of lycanthrope powers. But you will need to control the wolf inside you. I will endeavour to give you a helping hand in achieving the transformation for the first time, after which it should become much easier to bring it about yourself at will.

"Once you have transformed, we will fight. I want you to get an idea of what it feels like to come up against another nether-creature, and I can't think of a better one for you to cut your teeth on—please excuse that most unfortunate metaphor—than a vampire."

Lucien stopped then, his body posture suddenly becoming threatening and aggressive as he crouched slightly. There was a look in his eye that Trey didn't much like.

"Any questions?" Lucien asked, slowly moving to his right and starting to circle the teenager.

"Lucien, do we really have to do this? Isn't there some other way?"

"Now, it is crucial that you try to maintain control at all times during the next hour or so," Lucien continued, as if he had not heard him. "We will inevitably hurt each other during our sessions, and unlike the wounds that may be inflicted on us by humans—which will heal almost instantaneously—the wounds that nether-creatures inflict on each other are slow to heal. Should you lose control and attack me with the full force of tooth and claw, you could maim or even kill me. Do you understand, Trey?"

Lucien nodded toward the two corners that Tom and Hopper occupied. "That is the reason that they are here. They are my insurance against you losing control."

"What's my insurance against *you* losing control?" Trey asked.

"On that you will just have to place your trust in me again. Ready?"

"Lucien, I don't want to do this," Trey said.

"I know. If there was a better way, I would choose it. I expected this reaction, Trey. That's why I brought this." Lucien's eyes took on a cold, hard appearance and he curled his fingers around the handle of the baton in his hand, but

120

instead of raising it up over his head to strike the boy, he slowly extended his arm and pushed the end of it against Trey's chest.

The high-voltage, low-current shock from the cattle prod felt like a firebomb exploding inside Trey's chest. A tsunami of pain slammed through every molecule in his body, causing him to scream and stagger backward, falling to the hard floor. He couldn't get his lungs to work properly. The air that had been forced from his body with the violence of the shock would not return—panic started to grip Trey, until finally, after what seemed an age, his throat opened and he was able to suck in a ragged breath of air.

"Hurt, did it?" Lucien was behind him now, leaning over him, an evil sneer turning his face into a Halloween mask. His eyes blazed fiercely and he started to walk slowly toward Trey again. Trey looked over his shoulder and, for the first time since they met, saw beyond the calm, polished exterior that Lucien portrayed to the world, catching a glimpse of the nether-creature beneath. The vampire's face suddenly seemed incapable of pity and Trey was extremely glad that Lucien had chosen to have his fangs and claws removed all those years ago.

"Lucien . . ." Trey stammered at the advancing figure.

"You'd better get changing, Trey, because this thing's nearly fully charged again, and if you haven't changed by the time it's ready, I'm going to stick it on you again."

"My God, Lucien, what on earth do you think—"

"Too late, it's green-light-go time!" Lucien jabbed the

tips of the metal electrodes between the boy's shoulder blades.

Trey rolled across the floor in agony, the scream that escaped him sounding like a fox being torn apart by the hunting hounds. He rolled to a stop against Lucien's legs. Despite the curtains of pain that enveloped him, Trey couldn't understand how the vampire had got across the room so quickly to where he was now. The vampire moved with impossible speed.

He drew himself into a fetal ball and screamed at Lucien to stop.

Lucien lowered himself onto his haunches, looking down at the weapon in his hands. When he spoke again, his voice dripped poison. "I haven't tried this out on myself. I take it that it doesn't get any easier after the first one, then? You know, if you could just transform, all this could end. How about it?"

He paused for a second. "No? Shame, really, because this baby's nearly ready to go again. Ready for another, Trey?" He lowered the cattle prod toward the boy, the twin metal tips at the end of the pole ready to discharge their full force again.

"NO!" Trey roared, throwing himself away from his torturer and scrambling to his feet. A million supernovas exploded as tight, knotted balls of energy drew together and then detonated within him. It was a mixture of the most exquisite pain and the hugest adrenaline rush that he'd ever felt and it consumed him utterly. His body was rigid and stiff as every muscle in it locked, and he felt an uncomfortable pulling sensation deep inside his bones as they thickened and elongated. Muscle hypertrophied, the myofibrils within them multiplying exponentially, and he sensed the power that suddenly existed in his body. Thick, coarse hair erupted, covering his body from head to toe, and huge claws and fangs burst forth from his fingers and mouth.

His face was a freeze-frame of abject agony, jaw jutting forward, lips peeling back from his teeth in a kind of frantic sneer. To Trey it seemed to go on forever and he wondered why he had not passed out yet from the pain. To the others that watched, the transformation took less than a second.

And then nothing.

The chronic pain that he had tried to retreat from so utterly was gone as quickly as it had come. Trey opened his eyes and looked *down* at Lucien, who was standing looking up at him in an openmouthed expression of awe.

"Holy Mary, mother of God, will you look at the size of him?" Tom muttered from behind his barricade.

12

The monster in front of Lucien stood around seven feet tall. A deep-chested, wide-shouldered slab of muscle and bone that looked as if it weighed at least three hundred pounds. Gray-and-black fur covered it from head to toe, and a pale pink tongue lolled slightly from the mouth in the great wolf head. And teeth. There were so many teeth. The creature shook its head and stared at Lucien with yellow-and-orange eyes, the pupils of which were tiny pinpricks of black in the center.

Trey looked down at his body and flinched at the sight. He lifted one massive hand and turned it from front to back, puzzled to see that it was more human than he had expected. Rough pads had formed on his palms and between the joints of his fingers. He doubted he would be able to take up needlework as a werewolf, but he was surprised at the level of manual dexterity that he retained. He brought the hand nearer and examined the huge black claws protruding from the end of each digit. He raised the hand to touch his face.

Nothing about his head felt right. Large ears stuck out from the top of his head, and his *muzzle*—it was strange having to put names to body parts that, moments before, he hadn't even had—felt enormous. In a comedic gesture,

124

he daintily reached up with his forefinger and thumb and placed them around one of the huge canine teeth, running them up and down to gauge the size and length.

"There are full-length mirrors in the dance studio. You can take a good look at yourself shortly," Lucien said, looking up at him, a wide and genuine smile on his face.

Everything was too loud and too intense, as though the world had been hollowed out and the noises within it were bouncing around like bingo balls, jumbling and overlapping each other. But he also found that he could pick out the slightest noise and seem to isolate it from the rest of the cacophony, amplifying it and tuning out the surrounding hubbub. He could hear the fizzing of the tungsten filaments as they burned in the lightbulbs twenty feet above his head. He could hear Hopper and Tom breathing, openmouthed, in their corners. Outside the court he could discern the scritching sound of Alexa's cotton leggings rubbing against the seat fabric as she jiggled her leg up and down, anxiously watching the scene unfold.

Trey had never needed glasses, but looking at the world through werewolf eyes made everything seem so much sharper and more intense. It was too much. Too much information was registering, and his mind struggled to assimilate the sensory bombardment that it was being subjected to. He could pick out the individual pores on Lucien's face, the weave of the fabric on his tracksuit top. He also noted with a curiously detached interest that Hopper *shimmered.* Trey could see through the human exterior that Hopper wore in this world, and underneath Trey spied the real form of the demon, with its greedy eyes and wide, cruel mouth. The demon was looking back at him, its leathery eyelids flickering momentarily over the onyx-black globes that were its eyes. It flicked a snake-like tongue from between its lips as it studied him. Anxiously, Trey turned his head in Tom's direction and was relieved to see that Tom looked just like Tom.

But it was the smells that were the hardest to try to comprehend. They were everywhere and of everything and, like the sounds, they scrambled and clamored over each other, assaulting him from all directions. They were not just smells; they were intermingling colors and hues that stimulated a hitherto unused part of his brain to interpret them and provide feedback on their meaning. The purple of Lucien's aftershave was mixed with a leafy green aroma of fresh sweat, which was not unpleasant. Hopper stank of blackish-green dung that Trey had not the slightest recollection of detecting when they were first introduced. His own smell was quite different to how he had expected it to be; it was oaky and muddy like the smell that hits you when you newly open a bag of garden compost. And these smells were layered over the rubber-and-sweat color wash of the squash court itself, which Trey pictured as a light-brown haze.

"I can only imagine how you must be feeling at the moment, Trey," Lucien said in a quiet voice, breaking through Trey's thoughts. "It will simply be too much for you to take in all at once, but you must try to go along with it for a while longer." He took a step toward him and looked up with a crooked smile. "Now comes the dangerous part, Trey. Dangerous for me, that is, not you, because I will not hurt you in any way that will cause you any lasting damage. But you—well, everything is new to you. You must discover your power and speed, and how you can utilize them to your advantage. To do all this, we must fight. Try to maintain control. And do please try not to kill me, Mr. Laporte."

He stepped forward, jamming the cattle prod into Trey's stomach.

The pain was dialed right down. The high-voltage shock passed through him, and, yes, it still hurt like hell, but it was not in the same league as the torture the device had inflicted on him only moments before. It was like comparing an almighty kick in the head to being doused in petrol and set on fire.

As the charge hit him, Trey heard his new voice for the first time. It was an intense and guttural roar that escaped from deep inside him. In his mind he had shouted for Lucien to stop this madness, but these words were not the sounds picked up by his ears—instead he heard that lion-like bellow that echoed loudly around the walls.

"Are you just going to stand there and let me hit you with this again and again?" Lucien said. "Or are you going to try to do something about it?"

Snarls and growls replaced the pleas that he tried to

make, his inability to speak adding to the frustration and anger that Trey was experiencing.

"Perhaps you like it," Lucien continued. "Is that it, Trey? Is that why you stand there like some docile cow and allow me to hurt you like this?" Lucien sneered up at him, his eyes hard pools of fire in his contorted face. "Fine. If that's what you want." He feinted to his left, and then, shifting his weight quickly onto his right foot, he leaped toward Trey, aiming the tip of the cattle prod straight at his face.

Trey rocked back and instinctively threw up his right hand and grabbed the fiberglass rod halfway down its length. Snarling, he brought his left hand around toward Lucien's head; his fingers flexed, black-dagger claws scything the air.

But Lucien simply wasn't there. Trey swiped thin air, and his right fist, which had been holding the cattle prod, closed upon nothing. The searing pain in his right buttock announced exactly where the vampire had gone and he let out another roar of agony, rounding to face Lucien again.

Lucien tut-tutted and shook his head in disappointment. "Imagine," he said, "if I still had teeth and talons, you'd be lying dead in a pool of your own blood right now."

A new emotion stirred within Trey now. He felt the anger rising up inside him and he welcomed it, relishing the way that his new body responded to the adrenaline that coursed through him, feeding his already highly tuned senses. His muscles were bunched and tight as he eyed the vampire, looking for an opportunity to attack.

Trey lunged toward him, his lips pulled back to reveal rows of teeth sharp enough to shear through a man's arm. He hooked the thin air where Lucien had been standing a fraction of a second before and howled as he felt the pain once more course through him. This time, however, ignoring the pain, he pushed back against his front foot and shoulder-charged the area behind him that he guessed Lucien to be in.

The vampire smacked into the far wall with a satisfying thump and Trey was upon him. He launched himself through the air, aiming to land with both feet on his prone opponent. Instead, only the waxed wooden floor connected with his bare soles as, once again, Lucien misted.

There was something different this time, though. Trey noticed that the vampire appeared to flicker momentarily as he disappeared. From the corner of his eye, Trey caught a glimpse of that little flicker again, about six feet to his left, an eye-blink before Lucien reappeared in that very spot.

He's getting tired, Trey thought. *Either he can't mist for extended periods, or that crash into the wall has taken a lot out of him.*

"Better," Lucien said. "But you are still really only moving at half speed and you are too fixated on the pain. You need to learn to ignore the pain and concentrate on stopping the cause of it." He flipped his wrist against the leather strap, the cattle prod's handle jumping into his grasp. "Ready?" he said.

Trey didn't give Lucien a chance to come at him again. He ran at the vampire, closing the gap between them in an instant, and swung his arm around in a wide arc, knowing that he would not connect but being careful to maintain his balance as he waited for the right moment. He watched as Lucien misted again and was relieved to see that little flicker as he disappeared. This time Trey pivoted on his heel, watching for the telltale glimmer that would reveal where the vampire would appear next. He saw it no more than two feet away from him and thrust out his clawed hand just as Lucien rematerialized. He seized the vampire by the throat, catching hold of the cattle prod with his other hand. Pulling Lucien up off the floor toward him, he opened those huge jaws, a blast of hot breath hitting the vampire. Trey bellowed at Lucien and increased the pressure of his grip around his neck. A feeling of elation ran through him at the realization of his own power.—more power than he had ever felt before in his life. The vampire's face began turning from red to purple, and tiny blood vessels in his eyes popped, spilling their crimson cargo into their milky-white surroundings, but he made no attempt to break free from the life-threatening grip.

Tom and Hopper leaped up, but Lucien, catching sight of them out of the corner of his eye, raised his free hand to stop them.

"*Don't, Trey, please!*" Alexa's voice cut through the curtains of rage in Trey's mind. He could feel her anxiety as she witnessed her father hanging helplessly in his grasp and he remembered how Lucien had cautioned him against losing control.

He looked at Lucien's swollen face and relaxed the grip on his neck, the rage inside him slowly dissipating. He lowered Lucien to the ground and stepped back, panting, his tongue hanging from his mouth as he sucked in cool air.

"*Thank you,*" Alexa whispered in his head.

Lucien tenderly stroked his throat, looking up at Trey with a wide and admiring smile. Tom had moved up to stand behind his boss. Trey was surprised to see the vampire's reaction, and was suddenly filled with a great feeling of shame at the way that he'd allowed himself to lose control to the anger he had felt. He hung his head, taking in his huge and powerful body as he did so.

"Well, Mr. Laporte," Lucien said, "you really are quite something, aren't you?" He offered his hand like a boxer at the end of a contest. "You might want to transform back now, Trey. I think it's a safe bet to say that our training session is over for today."

"Jeez, I thought you were going to eat him!" Tom said, shaking his head and then laughing. "I didn't know whether to shoot this thing or run out and smash you over the head with it."

Trey closed his eyes and concentrated. There was a sucking feeling, as if every part of him was collapsing

131

into a central point within his abdomen—like being taken apart and put back together again. He tipped his head back and gasped, his eyes screwed shut against the pain and discomfort, which was intense but mercifully short. He opened his eyes again and took in the lights high up overhead on the ceiling, screwing up his eyes slightly and squinting as if trying to bring them into focus. Every part of him ached. It was a deep, disturbing feeling that seemed to emanate from the very marrow of his bones, making him shake all over. His throat was dry and he badly needed a drink. And he smelled. The odor was something akin to wet dog, and it filled the air around him.

He lowered his head and looked at Lucien, who proferred his hand again. Trey shook it and nodded toward the purple welt around the vampire's neck.

"Sorry if I—"

"Please, Trey, you don't need to apologize." Lucien cut him off. "Besides, compared to someone repeatedly electrocuting you with a few thousand volts, I think that this is small fry. How do you feel?"

"Now? Awful. Like a train wreck." He puffed out his cheeks and considered how to go on. "But when I was . . . that thing, I felt . . . exhilarated. Really alive, more alive than I have ever felt before. And the *power*, Lucien, it was incredible. When can we do it again?"

Lucien looked up at him, a smile playing at the sides of his mouth. "I think that we'll be able to put you through

132.

your paces with some other types of opponent over the next few days. There's a Nargwan demon in my employ called Luther. He's already agreed to come along and help you out, so we can schedule something for tomorrow, if you like?"

"No more cattle prods, though," Trey said, looking down at the weapon hanging from Lucien's wrist.

"Of course not. This was just a means to an end. I thought you might need some none-too-gentle persuasion to get you to morph for the first time." He reached out and placed a hand on Trey's shoulder. "I meant it, you know—you really are quite something. Of course, I still think that in my prime I would have been too much for you: I was *really* fast back then." Lucien smiled at him and then gave a small embarrassed cough. "You, er . . . you might want to get some clothes on."

Trey looked down in stunned disbelief as he realized that he was naked. He covered himself as best he could with his hands and looked around for his clothes. He saw them ruined and strewn across the floor.

"Perhaps you'd like me to send you some clothes down?" Alexa's voice cut in through his thoughts. *"I'll send down that pink-and-gray sweater that you liked so much."* Trey looked around to see her disappearing out of the door.

Trey gratefully accepted the towel that Tom offered him, wrapping it around his waist. The Irishman clapped his arm around Trey's shoulders. "We'll have to work something out about this whole 'clothing thing.' I think there might be a

133

solution in Lycra. Not very fashionable, but by God, it's stretchy as hell!"

"Where's Hopper?" Lucien asked.

They looked around to see that the demon had completely disappeared.

13

Trey slept for sixteen hours straight. When he woke up, it was a new day outside and he tensed as he rolled out of bed to open the curtains, expecting to ache and hurt all over. To his surprise, his body felt fine—he had none of the sore throat and aching head that he had had when he woke up that morning in his bedroom at Apple Grove. Looking at the bed, he realized that he'd slept on top of the covers, fully clothed. He'd changed into the clothes that Alexa had sent down for him and he still had on that awful pink-and-gray pullover. He sat down on the edge of the bed again and tried to piece together what had happened.

He didn't remember getting into bed. Hell, he didn't remember coming upstairs or coming into his room. In his mind, a thousand overlapping thoughts and emotions started to jostle and elbow for position again. He flopped back onto the bed and tried to take stock of everything that had happened to him in the last few days.

It was impossible for him to fix on any one point to start from—too much had happened too quickly, and every time he tried to piece things together in a sensible way, everything just tumbled in on him, turning his thoughts into a jumbled entropic mess. The inside of his head was like a DVD movie randomly skipping between scenes.

He shook his head as if to shake some sense into himself. He glanced down at his hands and pictured how they had looked only a day before. There was no indication that these very same fingers were capable of transforming into the terrible barbed weapons that he had tried to use on Lucien. He shuddered slightly at the idea of using those claws to harm anyone or anything, but when he had looked down at them through his wolf eyes, he'd reveled in the power in those hands, the power that had flooded every cell of him, and he knew that he was quite capable of using that power to destroy.

He stood up and crossed the room, noticing the small control panel set into the wall opposite his bed. He touched the screen and studied the opening menu of what appeared to be a multicontrol system for the apartment. Each room had its own lighting and temperature controls, as well as audio, video, and telecom functions. He pressed an icon and turned around to watch as the LCD screen slid down from a point in the ceiling opposite his bed. The screen disappeared again as he jabbed the button marked "audio," the control panel now showing a daunting selection of hi-fi options. By trial and error he managed to navigate through to the huge MP3 list that was no doubt stored on a central server somewhere else in the apartment. Someone clearly had great taste in music and had downloaded a number of his favorite bands' albums. He selected a track and pressed

Play, noticing for the first time the concealed speakers that were set at various points around the room. He took a deep breath and walked into his bathroom, noting how the music followed him.

I could get used to this kind of luxury, he thought as he turned the shower on and stepped inside. His thoughts returned to the image of the flames licking the roof of the care home, and he chastised himself for his selfishness.

After showering, he put on a huge fluffy bathrobe and decided to go and see if he could grab something to eat and drink.

There was an elderly lady in the kitchen busily wiping down the surfaces with a blue cloth, a kitchen spray held in her other hand. She turned slightly from her work to look at him, a warm smile replacing the look of concentration that she had worn as he entered.

"Hello, love," she said, without pausing in her work. "You must be Trey. Tom's told me all about you. I'm Mrs. Magilton, the housekeeper." She pumped the little handle on the bottle, sending a fine mist of pink liquid onto the marble worktop. "Now that you're up, I'll be able to get in to clean your room, if that's OK with you?"

"Sure," Trey replied, moving over to the fridge. He grabbed a carton of juice and a glass. He opened the door to the balcony and stepped out into the late-morning sunshine, squinting against the glare of the sun reflected off the water's surface. The river looked so different in the daylight—the water had lost the mystery that it had held when he had last stood here. Now it was merely a dull and murky body of water that carried along the silt it had churned up off to sea. He preferred the dark and cold look it had had when he and Lucien had stood looking at it before the sun came up.

He sensed someone behind him, but didn't turn. Instead he took a sip of the orange juice and continued to stare out at the river.

Alexa stood next to him and joined him in his silence.

"I feel like I've been asleep forever," Trey said eventually.

"You must have needed it. I imagine that it takes quite a bit out of you—especially the first time. How do you feel?"

"Amazingly good. I woke up expecting to feel like I'd been in a car crash, but I'm actually feeling pretty damn fine," Trey replied, shaking his head.

"Well, that's good, isn't it?" Alexa asked, detecting the unhappiness in his voice.

"Yeah, I suppose so."

There was another silence while they both contemplated the river again.

"What did it feel like?" Alexa asked.

Trey turned to look at her for the first time. She was wearing a white blouse and jeans and she had very little makeup on now. He thought how much nicer she looked without the "rock chick" face that she had worn when he first met her.

"Scary, painful, exhilarating, terrifying, astonishing. It

138

felt like nothing that anyone should feel. But you know, when I'd transformed and I stood there in front of your father for the first time as a werewolf, I felt *alive*. More alive than I've ever felt before. And that's the part that scares me, Alexa."

"Why?"

"Because I have to control this thing inside me. And if it feels that good to be a werewolf, what's to stop me wanting that all the time?"

She looked at him and smiled sadly, not knowing how to respond.

"Do you want to go shopping?" she asked suddenly.

"What? Have you just listened to what I said?" Trey shook his head and looked out at the view again. Everyone in this house was utterly screwed up. He'd just opened himself up to Alexa about things that were scaring the hell out of him, and she'd asked him if he wanted to *go shopping*.

"I think you need to get away from here for a while," Alexa said quietly. "I think you need some normality for a few hours. And when I want to forget stuff, I go shopping. Trust me, you'll feel a bit better having spent a few hundred quid of my dad's money—I always do. Besides, if you're going to get a taste for turning into a werewolf every two minutes, you're going to need loads of clothes."

Trey laughed. "OK, it sounds like a good plan. I *could* do with getting out into the real world again for a while. Who's going to ask him for the cash?"

"You. If I ask him, he'll send me off with a lecture about

mature spending ringing in my ears. He thinks I have a problem curbing my enthusiasm for clothes. *You'll* be able to get a huge wedge of cash out of him simply by telling him that you feel a bit down in the mouth and fancied getting out for some fresh air. Trust me: You need to ask for the dough."

"Where is he?" Trey asked.

"He'll be in his office. He was up all night and most of the morning trying to work out what happened to Hopper. He's worried—it's not normal for any of the nether-creatures to just up and disappear from Dad's organization. He'll also need to have had his daily top-up, if you know what I mean. He has the blood delivered here overnight, and he self-administers in his office."

She noticed the look on his face. "Don't worry, he'll have had it by now. You won't be walking in on him drinking blood or anything gross like that. He'll be all relaxed and . . . generous."

"OK, I'll go and ask. You sure it'll be all right?" Trey asked.

"He's loaded, Trey. Of course it'll be all right."

They walked through into the living area and over to the door leading to the reading room where on Trey's first night at the apartment Lucien had revealed the secrets about his past. Alexa pushed him gently toward the door. "The studded leather door in the rear wall," she said. "Best to knock first," she added, and went to sit in one of the recliners.

140

Trey knocked lightly against the wood surrounding the worn leather central panel of the door and was answered almost immediately by Lucien's voice inviting him to come in.

The door opened into a large, spacious office. To Trey's left was a bank of monitor screens, most of which were tuned into various news and business channels and Teletext pages. A huge wooden desk dominated the far wall, and it was behind this that Lucien sat, looking up at the boy as he entered the room. He stood up, the leather chair sliding back slightly on well-oiled casters.

"Trey, how are you today?" he asked. "I hope that you are rested?"

"Yes, thanks, Lucien. I still feel a bit odd about everything, you know; it's an awful lot to take in."

"Of course. But if you ever need a chat or if you have any questions at all, you only have to ask and I will do whatever I can to help."

Trey nodded. "Um, I was wondering if it would be OK to go shopping for some clothes, and Alexa said that I should—"

"Stop right there, Trey, please," Lucien said, holding up a finger to emphasize his request. He reached down to his side and opened what Trey assumed was a small cupboard door set into one of the desk's supporting columns. When he stood up again, Trey saw that he was holding the biggest bundle of banknotes that he had ever seen. Lucien held it out to him without even counting it.

"Lucien, that is a huge amount of money. I'm not sure I need all of—"

Lucien held up his finger again to stop him and dropped the money onto the desk. "Please sit down for a moment," he said, indicating a chair on the opposite side of the desk from him. He sat and smiled kindly at the teenager from behind a steeple that he had made from his hands.

"In the last few years, I have had to watch you face grief and cruelty from afar, and I have admired the way that you faced these things with courage and stoicism. I feel responsible for some of the suffering you have endured. If I now choose to buy you gifts and help you out in ways that I would have liked to have done before, you must indulge me." He paused and opened a drawer on his left, removing a large folder, which he placed on the desk. Opening this, he reviewed the front sheet and closed it again, sliding it across the desktop toward Trey.

"After your parents' deaths, I set up a trust fund for you. You have a fairly extensive portfolio consisting of gilt-edged bonds, shares, and properties in various countries. As of this morning, you are worth a little over one point two million pounds. Most of that amount is tied up at the moment, but I will happily sit down with you over the course of the next few weeks and we can decide what you want to do with your money."

Trey's mouth hung open as he looked from the man sitting behind the desk to the folder in front of him and back again.

142

"Besides," continued Lucien, "Alexa is a gold-medal Olympian when it comes to spending money, and I have very little doubt that she will help you to create quite a huge hole in this bankroll today." He nudged the wad of notes toward Trey and stood up.

Trey's mouth felt terribly dry. He stood up and moved toward the door. "Er . . . thank you. I mean . . ." His head was spinning again.

"Aren't you forgetting something?" Lucien called from behind.

He was holding out the stack of notes again. Trey took them, nodding his thanks before leaving. Outside, he sagged back against the closed door, trying to get his head around what Lucien had just told him. *One point two million pounds!* He closed his eyes and replayed the conversation in his head, trying to make sure that he had heard Lucien correctly. *One point two million pounds.*

As if he was not mentally in tatters already, Trey had the feeling that Lucien had just told him he was a millionaire.

14

"Where next?" Alexa asked as they turned away from the till. "Harvey Nics is not far from here. We could hop in a cab and be there in, like, no time."

Trey watched her fidgeting around on the spot with excitement like some demented dervish. They had been shopping for three hours now and she showed no signs of losing interest in the prospect of trawling through yet more rows of tagged and labeled clothing stretched out endlessly on silvered rails.

"I'm not really sure that I can take any more, Alexa."

"Nonsense," she replied. "You'll love Harvey Nics, and it really is not that far."

Nonsense, Trey was learning, was Alexa's favorite response to any comment that she didn't agree with. He had already heard it countless times that morning when he had protested about various items of clothing that she thought he should buy.

"I know what it is," she said. "You're still not sure about those linen trousers that I had you buy in Selfridges, are you?"

The escalator delivered them back to the ground floor of whichever department store this was—Trey had lost track, and they were all blurring into one huge mish-mash of chrome rails, overeager shop assistants, and curtained changing cubicles. The cloying, overlapping smells wafting over from the perfume and cosmetics counters suddenly made Trey desperate to find the doors and the reward of fresh air—if London's air could ever truly be described as fresh.

"To be honest, Alexa, I'm really not very sure about *most* of the stuff that you've had me buy."

"But that shop assistant agreed with me that they looked great on you." She tried one of her pouts on him, but Trey continued.

"Yeah, I heard that. I heard that right before she told me that they only cost one hundred and forty pounds. *And* I heard you tell her that we'd take them, along with those bloody awful shoes." They were outside now, standing on the corner of Oxford Circus. He tried to get her attention as she scanned the traffic for a black cab. "Alexa, I have never worn, and almost certainly never will wear, linen trousers. In fact, this will come as a bit of a blow to you, but I have managed to live almost my entire life with probably no more than three pairs of jeans, about twenty assorted T-shirts, sweats, and shirts, and a few pairs of sneakers at any one time."

The cab she tried to hail sailed right past, turning its large bulbous back on her like some black-bustle-wearing Victorian widow, too grand to acknowledge the hoi polloi daring to try to catch its attention.

145

"So what are you saying?" She huffed at the lack of cabs and started to walk slowly up the street, stopping every few strides at the merest flash of black appearing on the road up ahead.

He looked at her pouting face, and all the irritation that had been building up inside him boiled up to the surface. "Listen," he hissed. "My life has been turned upside down because of you and your family. Everyone I have ever cared for is dead. I only narrowly escaped being burned alive. Added to this, I've discovered that I am some kind of abomination of nature: a freak, a wolfman, and a potential killer. And to top it all"—his voice had risen so that the other shoppers openly stared at him now, giving the pair a wide berth—"you decide that what I really need is to be dragged miles around London to buy clothes that I wouldn't be seen dead in. Which is a situation that I have a feeling will come about all too soon—no thanks to the situation that your father has placed me in!"

Alexa stared at him for what seemed like forever. Her face was a mask of unreadable emotions. "Do you think you're the only one who has suffered in life?" she said finally. "Do you think that it's easy trying to grow up with a *vampire* for a dad? Trying to carve out a normal life for yourself when everything around you is anything but normal? You're not the only person to have lost someone. My mum died when I was very young too, so don't try and pull that 'I'm all on my own in all of this' line. I was *trying* to be nice to you." A small tear slipped from her right eye and snaked its way down her cheek. "I was trying to do something to help you forget the madness that you've been living for the past few days. I wish I hadn't sodding well bothered."

"So go home, then!" Trey shouted at her.

During this outburst she'd stood by the edge of the road, keeping her hand held out to hail a taxi. Just then, one of the giant black cabs pulled in beside her, the loud, staccato nagging of its diesel engine filling the air around them both.

"I'll do that." She opened the door of the taxi, adding, "You're a selfish, spiteful, ungrateful pig, Trey Laporte." And with that, she piled into the back of the vehicle, dragging assorted bags in with her. The taxi pulled off into the traffic. Trey stood and watched it disappear up the road, noticing through the rear window how Alexa had placed her head in her hands and started to cry again.

15

Trey stood in the street for what felt like hours, the few bags that Alexa had left behind still scattered at his feet as people eddied around him, the numbers of shoppers slowly becoming fewer as the evening drew in and the shops started to close. He thought about what Alexa had said, and now that his anger had abated, he couldn't find any fault in her arguments. He had been selfish and cruel. Perhaps he *had* become too self-obsessed. And yet it was hard for him to imagine how he could have gone through everything he had in the last few days and *not* be self-obsessed. He kept seeing the single tear that had escaped her eye and traced a course down the flesh of her cheek. She had been the one person who had really helped him keep it together, and he regretted taking it out on her in the way that he had.

Eventually, he became aware of the strange looks that he was getting from the people passing by and turned and walked aimlessly down Regent Street, leaving the little island of shopping bags for some fortunate street dweller to find that evening—they didn't seem important anymore. He was walking past the department store Liberty when he remembered that it was the only shop that he and Alexa had been in that day where she had lingered over any item of clothing for herself—she'd even gone as far as trying it on before dragging him off to the menswear department. He needed to apologize to Alexa, and he thought he knew the ideal way to do it.

Fifteen minutes later, Trey left the store and walked out into the cold winter evening. The temperature had dropped quickly during his time in the store, and he pulled his jacket around him and looked for a taxi. The dress was now beautifully wrapped in tissue paper and the assistant had put it into a box and tied the whole thing around with a deep purple ribbon that had the store's name printed on it in white. He walked a long way north along Regent Street, silently pleased with himself and working out in his head how he was going to put things right with Alexa. The box knocked against his calf as he walked, but he ignored it and everything else around him as he played the scene over in his head, practicing his apology and trying to figure out how she might respond.

Eventually he realized that he'd walked past all the shops and entered Portland Place, approaching Regent's Park up ahead. There were far fewer taxis going past now, and far fewer people in the street, which was dominated by the foreign embassies of various countries. Those cabs that did come along ignored his attempts to hail them, sailing past him, ferrying people back to their centrally heated homes and away from the cold city air. He paused for a second

149

and debated walking back again to increase his chances of getting a taxi when he saw one coming toward him. He quickly moved to the curb and put his arm up, leaning out so that the driver would see him.

He didn't hear the footsteps behind him until it was too late. One of the youths slammed into him, knocking him off balance, the other ripped the bag out of his hand, and the two of them were off, sprinting up the street toward the park. Trey managed to stay on his feet, avoiding slipping off the curb into the path of the oncoming taxi, but when he looked up again, the two boys already had a thirty-meter head start on him. He took off after them, breaking into a sprint to keep them in sight.

Trey's long legs ate up the pavement as he hurtled after the pair. He could see them ahead of him, and he began to close the gap on them as they slowed slightly. They never looked behind them to see if anyone was following, and Trey guessed that they must have done this kind of thing before and that they assumed that with the element of surprise and a good head start, most people simply would not give chase. At the top of Portland Place they ran around the semicircle of Park Crescent and disappeared down the steps leading to Regent's Park underground station.

Trey had to turn sideways to squeeze through the gap in the sliding iron gate that should have been fully open at the entrance to the station from the street. It briefly registered with him that this was odd, but, almost losing sight of the two thieves at the bottom of the stairs, he pushed the thought away and followed them down, taking the stairs three at a time, just in time to see the second boy jump over the ticket barrier and head toward the escalators that led down to the Bakerloo Line. Trey thought it odd too that there was no guard on duty and no people in the ticket area of the station. Then he remembered: Regent's Park station was closed. There were signs up all over the ticket concourse with information on the station's closure. It had been shut for months now and was due to be closed for another three or four while the station was refurbished. He grinned as he too leaped over the barrier and headed toward the stationary escalators, knowing that as long as he could keep these two in sight, there was no way that they were going to escape him.

He looked ahead, increasing his speed down the rutted metal steps of the escalator, and watched the two boys jump over a fold-out barrier that had been erected in front of the tiled corridor that led to the Bakerloo Line. Trey cleared the ineffectual gate, just catching his trailing foot on the NO ENTRY placard that had been set up on top of it, causing it to crash loudly to the ground behind him. Up ahead he heard a tube train hurtle through the station. No trains had stopped here for months; they tore through at full speed, giving the passengers on board the briefest of glimpses at the work being carried out on the platforms and entrances. Trey was surprised that his muggers had not known this when using the station as a means of escape. Or maybe they *had* known

151

and deliberately used this as a getaway, assuming that few people would be willing to follow them down here through the dark and deserted corridors of a closed station.

He slowed momentarily at the bottom of the walkway, confronted with a choice of platforms: eastbound or westbound. He guessed at one and walked toward the westbound platform, deciding to check that first.

He guessed correctly. The two teenagers were standing just up from the entrance to the platform. They were breathing hard and looking back in his direction as he came through the opening.

Trey stood with his hands by his sides. He too was out of breath, and he eyed the two teenagers carefully while he pulled the stale, dirty air of the underground into his lungs, getting his breathing back to normal.

"I think that you've got something of mine," Trey said.

"Oh really?" said the youth nearest to him. "What might that be, then?" He had peroxide-blond hair that was cropped close to his scalp, and one side of his upper lip curled slightly and ran into a scar that led up toward his nose. Trey guessed that the disfigurement was the result of surgery on a cleft palate. The teenager angled his head to one side and jutted his jaw forward in a look that Trey thought was supposed to be hostile. He reminded Trey of a dog that used to live in a house near the care home. Whenever anyone walked near the wire fence that ran down the side of the house, the little dog would run up to it, snarling and baring its fangs in an open show of aggression.

His colleague was slightly shorter, with shoulder-length black hair that he had shaved down both sides to reveal the blue-black skull tattoos on his scalp above his ears. It was Tattoos who had Trey's bag in his hands.

Trey guessed that they must both be about the same age as him, although he was taller and heavier than both of them.

"My bag," Trey said, nodding in the direction of the smaller boy.

"And what makes you think this is your bag?" asked Harelip.

"You mean besides the fact that I just followed you down here after you snatched it out of my hand? How about this: It's got *my* stuff in it, so hand it over. Besides," he added, trying to dispel some of the tension, "it's got a dress in it, and I don't think the color is going to suit either of you."

"Why don't you come and get it?" Harelip snarled, pulling a nasty-looking knife out of his jacket pocket. He raised one eyebrow, a thin, mean smile playing at his lips. "Or maybe you've had a rethink and worked out that it isn't your bag after all?"

Trey looked at the knife held tightly in the boy's hand, and then moved his eyes slowly upward to look into the faces of the two thieves. "I'll give you one more chance to hand me back my bag and walk away from here while you still can. Because, believe me, if you don't, you two are going to see something that'll make you wet your bed every night for the rest of your lives."

"Get a load of him," snarled Harelip. "Fancy yourself as a bit of a tough nut, do ya?"

"You've no idea, Scarface," Trey replied.

"Get him!" said Tattoos. He dropped the bag and lunged toward Trey, balling his right hand into a fist and cocking it by his shoulder.

Trey morphed. One second he was a five-foot-eleven, fourteen-year-old teenager—the next a seven-foot, barrel-chested, angry, snarling werewolf.

And in the spilt second it took him to transform, Trey realized that it was an ambush.

The two demons moved incredibly quickly. They were squat powerful-looking creatures that looked as if they were made of pure muscle. Their inky-black bodies seemed to shimmer as if a black flame burned across the surface of their skin, gobbling up all the available light. Their mouths were ghastly slits, the thin, greedy lips rolled back over sharp, jagged black teeth arranged on the gums in three uneven rows, like lines of pike-wielding soldiers readying for attack—their combatants-in-arms ranked behind them, ready to fill in any gaps made in the line. Their eyes consisted of densely packed clusters of small black globes, sinister and baleful bunches of hate-filled berries that had never reflected back anything but malevolence and contempt.

Tattoos had leaped from its feet and was flying toward him. It slammed its fist into Trey's cheekbone, instantly reaching forward with its other hand, trying to hook a clawed thumb into Trey's left eye socket. Trey twisted his head to one side and swiped his clawed fingers at the demon's body, missing by a fraction. He kicked out with his left leg as Harelip came running toward him with the knife, catching the demon in the midriff and sending the air out of its lungs with a great "Ungghf!"

Tattoos landed softly on the balls of its feet. Its wide, ugly mouth stretched back over those teeth in what Trey guessed must be something that passed as a smile. Trey stepped back slightly so that he could keep both of them in his field of vision.

Harelip was similar-looking to Tattoos, except that the entire middle section of its face was missing. A black hole existed where its nose and upper lip would have been, and it seemed to Trey that it should have been impossible to survive a wound like that.

The demons moved toward him from each side. They inched forward slowly, their eyes intent on him, waiting to make their move.

Trey wasn't about to let them both rush him. He had already decided that Tattoos was the more dangerous of the two, but he really didn't relish the idea of Harelip tearing toward him with that long, curved blade in its hand. He feinted toward Tattoos, and then spun around on Harelip as the demon came at him, raising the knife. Trey sank his teeth into the demon's outstretched forearm, pulling the creature up off its feet and shaking it in the air until the knife clattered to the ground.

Tattoos sprang up onto Trey's back and sank its own teeth into his shoulder, biting down hard with needle-sharp fangs. The demon reached around, trying to claw Trey's face, but its hands were intercepted by Trey's own and grasped in the werewolf's powerful grip. Trey felt the demon's teeth still clamped onto the flesh around his collarbone as Tattoos bit down harder to inflict the maximum amount of pain.

"Do something, Shnirop!" screamed Harelip, kicking out against Trey's huge body, its clawed feet raking great gouges where they connected. "He's going to bite my friggin' arm off if you don't do something!"

Trey heard the train approaching way before the demons did. His werewolf hearing was amazingly acute and he guessed that the train must be approaching at full speed as it raced along the tunnel toward them.

Just then, Tattoos shifted its weight on Trey's back and raised its legs up at the knees on either side of Trey's body. The demon planted its feet against the werewolf's hips and released its bite on his shoulder.

Trey guessed what it was planning—the demon had raised itself higher in order to deliver a killer bite to Trey's neck, to sink those merciless, razor-sharp teeth through his carotid artery and put an end to him.

The train arrived just in time, bursting free of the black tunnel and filling the empty platform with a tidal wave of sound. Trey knew what he had to do. He released his vise-like hold on Harelip's arm just as the train was about to draw

156

level with them and kicked the demon away from him. The creature flew straight into the path of the speeding train, and Trey saw it hit the windows in front of the horrified driver seconds before the train entered the tunnel at the other end of the station. He felt the other demon on his back and threw his entire body against the tiled wall behind him, crushing Tattoos with his weight and knocking the breath out of the nether-creature. He spun on the pads of his right foot and raked a huge, rending tear across the demon's throat, turning his own head to try to avoid the hot fountain of black gore that spewed onto him from the demon's already dead body.

The piercing squeal of the train's brakes against the rails as the driver executed his emergency stop knifed through Trey's head. He quickly looked up and saw that the people in the final carriage of the train were staring back toward him in wide-eyed horror as they glimpsed what appeared to be a giant werewolf standing on the platform of a London Underground station.

Fortunately, by the time the train finally came to a halt, it was entirely inside the tunnel to his right and Trey was obscured from sight. He looked down at where the dead body of the demon lay and saw that it was starting to fade. He watched until it had disappeared completely.

I've got to get out of here, thought Trey, his mind racing now that the fight was over. *I need to become human and get the hell out of here before this place is crawling with police.*

He morphed back to his human form and stared down at his naked, bleeding body. Deep cuts to his legs and abdomen wept blood freely and the gash under his eye was also bleeding profusely. As soon as he had transformed, the pain of the cuts could be felt to their full effect—his human nerve endings shrieking at the damage done to them. He looked down at the clothing that had moments before housed the shimmering black body of the demon and noted that there was no blood on them. There was nothing to suggest what outrages had been perpetrated on the body that had inhabited those garments moments before. He reached forward and picked up the tracksuit jacket, pulling it on over his naked torso and grimacing as he fastened the zipper, aware that seconds before, it had been sodden with the demon gore. But it was perfectly dry now. The blood, like the demons, had disappeared. Besides, Trey couldn't afford to be too picky right now. He pulled on the tracksuit bottoms, and even considered trying the shoes on, but quickly realized that they would not even come close to going over his feet.

On unsteady legs he walked over to where the Liberty bag had been thrown to the floor. He picked it up and, checking inside, was strangely relieved to see that the foul nether-creatures had not damaged the package that he had bought for Alexa.

He left the station without remembering climbing the same deserted steps that he had run down shortly before. He was panicked, and his heart thumped in his chest.

He'd just killed. He had just taken a life. No matter that they were not human and he was in mortal danger himself; he had just killed those things with his bare hands.

The same London streets greeted him: The same air, the same sickly street lighting, the same petrol-choked smell of the city assaulted his olfactory senses. But something had changed. Something that was more *him* than anything that was around him had changed forever, and he sensed that there was no way of ever going back to how things had been before.

He walked along, glancing down at the clothing that he had taken from the dead creature only moments before, and noticed how the bloodstains from his own wounds were now soaking through the material, appearing black in the orange light cast from the overhead streetlamps. He touched the sticky fluid, knowing that while he was in no mortal danger—the cuts and gouges were deep but not life-threatening—the continuous loss of blood could cause problems soon enough if he did not get some treatment. He looked around him and was surprised to find that he had stumbled along without thinking and had entered the park, so that he was now standing about twenty meters inside the perimeter fence.

The air smelled cleaner here, the grass releasing its nighttime perfume into the air and masking the worst of the city's stench. A large oak tree grew to his left, its ancient branches hanging out over him like the bony outstretched appendages of some great spider that had stopped and frozen, caught in the act seconds before it was about to reach down and grab him and sweep him up into some unseen hungry maw.

Trey looked up between the branches at the sky and the myriad stars that blinked their light at him from unimaginable distances, and he felt the overwhelming urge to morph into his wolf self again. Part of this desire was the knowledge that he would not feel a fraction of the pain that was gnawing at his human body now, but the greater part of him knew that he would feel *alive* out here in this great open space, running beneath the night's canopy, his wolf senses taking in the smells and sights and sounds of everything around him. But over and above this strange compulsion was the instinctive knowledge that he must not give in to these urges, that he must control these feelings at this early stage of his powers, so he pushed the thoughts away, pushed them back down deep inside him.

His thoughts turned again to the two demons that had lured him into an ambush, and he remembered the look on their faces as he had killed them, trying to save his own life. He recalled the bitter, metallic taste of their blood in his mouth, and then shook his head in disgust as a rogue thought knifed its way into his consciousness.

It had tasted good, some alien voice seemed to whisper in his mind, and he fought against a wave of nausea that threatened to make him sick.

It hadn't tasted good, he told himself. It had been revolting and terrible.

He was shaken from these thoughts by the sound of the shopping bag hitting the floor, having slipped out of his hand. He looked down at it and frowned slightly, as though seeing it for the first time. He bent down and picked it up again, noting the drip of blood that splashed against its surface as he did so.

He needed to get away from here, away from the area around the station and to safety.

Stumbling out of the park's exit gate again, he tried to hail a taxi that was passing by. The driver slowed down and swung in toward him before quickly speeding up again and accelerating away upon noticing the bloody mess that was the boy's clothing.

Alone, bleeding, and scared, Trey did the only thing he could: He found a phone box and called Lucien, asking him to come and rescue him.

16

Tom had dressed Trey's wounds as best he could in the back of the car on the journey home. He worked in the sparse light given out by the car's cabin light, applying bandages around the boy's body after doing his best to disinfect and seal the wounds with Steri-Strips.

"That should hold you together until we can get a doctor to look at you," he said, patting Trey on the arm and sitting next to him.

Lucien drove through London in silence. He'd not asked any questions on the way home, except to inquire if Trey was OK and to ask if Tom felt that they should take him to a hospital. Trey was unsure whether it was anger or worry that kept the tall vampire from asking what had happened to him, but once they had parked in the garage and Lucien came around to help Tom in getting him upstairs, the look of concern on his face and the way he spoke to Trey as they assisted him into the elevator put the teenager's mind at rest. Lucien had called ahead from the car, checking with Alexa if the doctor was on his way, and when the elevator doors opened, Trey saw a strange little man waiting alongside Alexa and assumed that he was the medical help that Lucien had alluded to.

Lucien and Tom supported him on either side, their arms linked through his in case he should fall. Trey leaned heavily into Lucien. His head was swimming and the room began to tilt alarmingly as he struggled to maintain his focus.

"I'm sorry, Lucien," he managed to mumble. He thought that he might throw up on the thick cream carpet that covered the floor and closed his eyes momentarily to try to regain some equilibrium.

Alexa hurried over to them as soon as the elevator doors opened. Her eyes had a pink, puffy look, as though she had been crying, and despite his pain and discomfort, Trey thought she looked prettier than ever: vulnerable and delicate. He smiled up at her and nodded his head, trying to communicate to her that he was all right. He thought that he just might be falling in love with her.

A blackness that had been creeping around at the edges of his vision quickly rushed in and blanked out the world as Trey lost consciousness.

When he came to, Trey was in his bed, and Tom was asleep in a chair by his bedside. The Irishman was snoring quietly and Trey grinned at the sound. His new friend had a book in his lap, but from his prone position Trey couldn't see the title. He tried to sit up to get a better look and his body lit up in a firework display of pain. It was impossible to pinpoint exactly which part of him hurt the most— stiletto blades of pain twisted within him from every angle.

163

The little groan that escaped him was enough to wake Tom from his slumber.

"I'm guessing you've worked out that lying down is the best bet right now," Tom said, that lopsided grimace of a smile contorting his face. "You'll be more full of scars than me if you carry on fighting with Shadow demons on your own like that." He paused and nodded his head. "How are you, lad?"

"To be honest, I've felt a whole lot better, Tom."

The bedroom door opened and Alexa's head appeared around the jamb. "Can I come in?" she asked. "I heard voices and I thought I'd come and see if he was awake." She smiled sadly at Trey and waved at him with the tips of her fingers as she entered.

"I'll go and get you something to drink," Tom said, exiting and leaving the two of them alone.

As soon as he had gone, Alexa turned to Trey, her face etched with concern. "I'm so sorry, Trey. This is my fault. If I hadn't left you in the middle of London like that, this would never have happened. I really am—"

"Don't be so stupid, Alexa," Trey cut through her. "If I hadn't spoken to you like a total jerk, I wouldn't have been on my own in London. Besides, those guys were waiting for an opportunity to get to me. They weren't hanging around by chance—they ambushed me, and I fell for it, like an utter idiot." He held up his hand to stop her again. "To be honest, Alexa, I'm glad you weren't around when it happened; it wasn't a very pretty thing to witness." His voice had gone all small and thin, and he looked up at the ceiling, clamping his teeth together hard, trying to stop the tears that welled up in the corners of his eyes. He wiped them away with the back of his hand, hissing at the pain that this simple act caused him.

Turning his head toward her again, he asked, "Do you think you could help me get out of this bed?"

"The doctor said that you were to rest." She paused, then added, "You've been *asleep* for two days, Trey."

He held his breath for a second while he took this in. He'd wondered why they had felt it necessary for Tom to babysit him overnight, but the revelation that he had been unconscious for two days made him realize that perhaps they'd thought he was going to die, and decided to post a vigil by his bedside just in case.

"My father and Tom have been taking it in turns to sit with you. Dad's hardly been out of your room. In between sitting with you, we have been looking into what happened. The information that we've managed to gain from our people inside Caliban's organization would suggest that you're right: The demons were sent specifically to try to take you out, Trey." She chewed her bottom lip and flicked her eyes down to the bandages around his chest and abdomen. "We know that they were Shadow demons. But we haven't been able to track either of them down yet, but when my father does . . ."

"You won't find them, Alexa. They're dead . . . I killed them." Trey looked away from her, turning his head so that she wouldn't see his face.

Alexa reached out and took hold of one of his hands in both of hers. "I'm so sorry, Trey. It must have been horrible. I can't imagine how you must feel."

When Trey turned to face her again he saw that she was crying, and the sight of her tears sparked a memory in his head of that night. "Where's my bag?" he said.

"Bag? What bag?"

"Don't tell me that I didn't have it with me when your dad picked me up? I had a bag with me when I left the station."

There was a knock on the door and Lucien came in. The smile that spread across his face when he looked at Trey filled the teenager with an odd mixture of happiness and guilt. He thought about the way that he'd treated Lucien up until now, and how he had done nothing to thank him for the kindness and care that his guardian had shown him.

"So, you're awake? Excellent. We were getting a bit worried about you for a while there. How are you feeling, Trey?"

"Sore, beaten-up, stupid, and strangely emotional, like the least thing is going to set me off into floods of tears," Trey said with a smile. "But I'm guessing that I'd feel a whole lot worse if it hadn't been for you, Lucien. Thank you . . . for everything."

Lucien nodded his acknowledgment and crossed the room to pull the curtains open.

"I'd like to get up," Trey said, as the sunlight poured into the room.

"I really wouldn't recommend that right now," Lucien replied.

"I'd like to get up, Lucien," Trey said with more emphasis, and after a moment Lucien nodded. He moved around to the side of the bed that Alexa was standing by, looming over the prone figure on the mattress.

"We'll see how you do. If you start to feel faint or sick, we'll bring you straight back. Now, will you try to stand or would you like me to carry you?"

Trey looked up at him and realized that he was quite serious. "I'll walk, if it's all the same with you."

He held his breath as Lucien helped him up onto his feet, trying to ignore the signals of hurt that his body fired off in volleys to his brain. He held his breath again once he was upright and tenderly felt the area around his stomach with his fingertips.

"I'm hoping that's the worst bit over with," he said.

He walked through to the living room after Lucien and Alexa had helped him into his bathrobe, ignoring the disapproving scowls that Tom shot in his direction when he saw that he was up and about. Sinking into one of the chairs, he blew out the breath that he had been holding during the short journey, and managed a smile up at the three faces surrounding him.

"A cup of tea would be nice," he said.

"Lucien," he went on, as Tom went over to put the kettle on, "where's the bag that I had with me when you picked me up? I *did* have a bag with me, didn't I?"

"Yes, you did," his guardian replied. "It's in your bedroom near the window."

"Alexa, would you like to get it?" he asked, relieved to know that it had been fetched back along with him and that it was still safe. It was strange how important he felt that bag to be. It was as if deep down he'd attached a symbolic status to it, and the news that it was still in his possession filled him with a happiness that was at odds with the value or importance of its contents.

Alexa came back carrying the Liberty bag. She placed it on the table, frowning at Trey.

"Open it, Alexa, it's for you," he said, smiling. "I had to go through quite a bit to get that back here in one piece, so I hope you like it."

Tom placed a steaming mug of tea in front of him and they watched as Alexa pulled the ribbon from the box and lifted the lid. She gasped when she saw the dress within, and looked up at him with a smile that made his chest tighten and the blood race around his body just a little faster.

"It's a present," he said. "Well, more of an apology really. I wanted to say sorry for the things that I said to you the other night—I had no right to treat you like that." He turned to face Lucien. "It's all right, isn't it? To buy it for Alexa with the money that you gave me?"

"It was your money, Trey. You can choose to spend it how you like," Lucien replied.

"I'd like to thank you all for the kindness that you've shown me," Trey said after taking a sip of the hot, sweet tea.

168

"I've been a bit of a jerk, and I don't think that I've given you all a fair chance really. It's been a bit hard for me . . . coming to terms with everything, but I know that you've all been trying to make it as easy for me as possible, and I'm grateful to you. Thank you."

The phone rang on the wall and Tom moved over to pick it up, listening to the person on the line before replacing the handset. "That was Charles from downstairs—they've picked up a signal from the Ring of Amon. It looks like Caliban is going to use it as we suspected."

Trey had no idea what the message was supposed to mean, but judging from the looks that passed among the other three people during the silence that followed, he was willing to bet that it was something very, very bad.

17

Tom dug around in a cupboard and produced a packet of doughnuts that he placed on the table along with Trey's second mug of hot tea. He had helped Trey to move into the kitchen, and Trey thought it odd how this man, whom he had thought of as harsh and brusque, seemed to fuss around him far more than his injuries really merited.

Alexa had rushed off downstairs following the telephone call, and Lucien explained to Trey that she had been researching this Ring of Amon for some time now and that she would need to see the new data.

The three of them spoke openly about the attack on Trey at the underground station, and Trey described the fight that he had had with the two demons. Lucien kept stopping him and asking him questions about specifics that Trey had thought were unimportant at the time. But the vampire sat in silence as Trey described how he had killed the two demons and how their dead bodies had simply disappeared in front of his eyes.

"Their bodies would have turned up in the demon world," Tom explained. "Although from what you say about Harelip getting splattered all over the front of the tube train, I don't suppose an awful lot of *him* would have turned up."

Tom looked over at Lucien and raised an eyebrow. "Tough as old boots, this one," he said, nodding his head in Trey's direction.

"I thought we'd established that the other day during our training session," Lucien replied, smiling back at the Irishman.

Tom screwed his right eye up. The overall effect, with the huge ugly scar on that side of his face, reminded Trey of something out of a zombie film he had once watched. "Ah, but *then* he was just fighting an old fart like you. Taking out two *young* Shadow demons takes some doing, I might suggest."

Trey looked at the two figures on either side of him and realized that Tom was teasing Lucien, hoping to get a reaction.

Instead, Lucien picked up his tea and finished off the remains from the bottom of the mug. His eyes glinted with amusement over the top of the ceramic rim.

Realizing that Lucien was not going to rise to the bait, Trey felt stangely obliged to defend him a little. "Lucien's not that old, Tom. What are you, Lucien? Forty? Forty-five tops."

Lucien lowered the cup and his smile broadened as he held Tom's eyes. It was his turn to raise an eyebrow. Eventually he turned back to Trey. "I'm almost two hundred and twenty years old, Trey. But thank you. Some people have natural tact and diplomacy, some do not," he said, nodding in the direction of the Irishman.

"Bet you feel bad now, don't you, Trey?" Tom said, a glint in his eye suggesting that he was not quite done yet. "Beating up on a poor old decrepit man like you did. The youth of today—bloody disgrace." He grinned and tousled the boy's hair, standing up to clear the cups from the table.

Trey stared again at the vampire sitting by his side, amazed at this latest revelation that had been dropped on him.

Lucien looked over at him and, as if reading his thoughts, smiled and added, "Think of it as a kind of dog's years, but for vampires."

"What happened to Hopper the other day, Tom?" Trey asked after another long pause.

"That is a question that I have been asking myself since our little friend disappeared," he said, moving over to the kitchen to put the cups into the sink. "None of our people have managed to locate him, and demons wandering around in the human plane are usually easy to trace. He's completely disappeared off the radar."

"I think it is safe to assume that we unwittingly invited a rat into our camp," Lucien said. "And that said rat is working for my brother, Caliban. If that is indeed the case, there is no doubt in my mind that my brother will have been responsible for setting those goons onto Trey the other day in an attempt to kill him."

Tom nodded and glanced at his employer. "Hopper came highly recommended from one of our people, Lucien. I swear to you that if we had even the slightest inkling that there was anything untoward, we would never have used him."

Lucien held up a hand to stop him. "Nobody is blaming you, Tom. I know how careful you are when choosing personnel. It does not change our plans, but it may add to the urgency of the matter. Caliban will definitely use the ring sooner now."

"What ring?" Trey said.

"The Ring of Amon," Lucien answered. "It's an ancient artifact from the Netherworld. It was believed to have been destroyed a very long time ago. The ring, when used in conjunction with a particular incantation, has the power to change people: It reverses their moral compass, and makes normal people do things that they would never have contemplated before falling under its spell. The ring has the power to unlock all the potential for rage and evil that people have. Normal people—good people—will commit acts of vile butchery on those around them, even those they love and hold dear. We think that Caliban hopes to use the ring to turn humankind against itself. And when he has done so, he wishes to create a vampire dynasty within the realm: a vampire empire with himself as ruler."

"If he's as powerful as you say he is," said Trey, "why doesn't he just walk in anyway? What does he need the ring for?"

Lucien glanced at Tom and a smile momentarily flashed across his features before disappearing again. "Human beings are a particularly obstinate species when it comes to their subjugation. In the past, Caliban and others like him have sought to bring the human world to its knees by destabilizing the people of Earth through wars, disease, and famine. The ring is the perfect weapon to create a state of chaos and break the human spirit."

"They want to wipe out humanity?"

Lucien looked at Trey, considering how best to respond. "No, Trey, they do not want to destroy humanity. In fact, quite the opposite. We vampires *need* humans. We have existed in this world for as long as anyone can remember, feeding on the blood of the living to guarantee our own survival. For century upon century we did this without discovery. We were the rulers of the night. But we got careless. We became complacent and the humans discovered the truth about our kind. They learned that we were not invincible and they learned that we could be killed. Our numbers, never great, dwindled as we were hunted down and destroyed. We hid in the Netherworld, only venturing into the human realm to feed, and dreamed of a day when we could return." He turned his head and looked out of the window. "The ring could make that dream a reality: a limitless food source that is broken, that lacks the coordination to fight back against those that seek to feed upon it. For my brother it is a dream, for the rest of us, a nightmare."

Trey looked between the two men, trying to take this in.

"We had a tip-off," Tom said, "from one of our people

who is working inside Caliban's organization, telling us that he had somehow acquired the ring. At first we were not too concerned and believed that the damage would be minimal—as Lucien says, the ring bearer must be heard by anyone that he wishes to convert. But then we discovered that he intended to use it in conjunction with mobile-phone networks. A technology-embracing, modern-day monster is Caliban. He has friends in high places in all the mobile networks throughout the world, and we believe that he might be able to broadcast simultaneously to every telephone number on any particular network. He plans to try a dry run in Amsterdam next month."

"Why Amsterdam?" asked Trey.

Tom shrugged and said, "Why not? To Caliban, one place is as good as another, but west Holland has the highest level of mobile-phone ownership in Europe. If you were going to try to use the ring in this way, I can't think of a better place to use as a test bed."

Lucien stood up and walked to the window. "If he succeeds, Amsterdam will turn into a living hell for its inhabitants. Whole families will be wiped out by the very people that they love.

"Our sources tell us that he intends to use Holland as an experiment and, depending on the level of success, will then use the ring around the world to spread death and misery across every continent. Earth will become a hell where the evil that vampires do will be as nothing compared to what man will do to man."

Lucien studied the floor for a moment before adding, "As a strategy, this is not entirely unprecedented. Many rulers of the Netherworld have sought to destabilize the human world in order to take it over for themselves. For the vampires it has always been about blood, but for others it has been the very souls of mankind that they sought. There hasn't been a dictatorship, war, or massacre on Earth that they have not had some part in. But with the ring, used in the way that he intends to, I fear that my brother will finally bring those who would defy him and his kind to their knees."

"He has to be stopped," said Trey.

"Yes, he does." Lucien turned from the window and looked at him. "But there is something else, Trey, something that concerns your personal safety. We have been helping to 'shield' you since your arrival here. Alexa has the ability to mask the telltale signature signs that are created when you transform. Caliban would have assigned a number of the people in his employ to look out for any such signs, just in case he hadn't succeeded in killing you in the fire the other night. My brother believes that you are a great threat to him. He knows how your powers will continue to grow as you mature, and as the murderer of your parents, Caliban is naturally concerned that you will one day seek revenge for their deaths. And then there is the matter of the Theiss legend." He held his hand up to stop Trey's protests. "My brother has made up his mind that he wants you dead, Trey, and he will stop at nothing to get to you and make sure that happens."

176

"What can I do, Lucien? If he's as powerful as you have said, and he knows that I am here, surely it is just a matter of time before he gets to me."

"We had hoped that we could keep you hidden from him until you were stronger and more prepared. He knows that if he can get at you before you have full control over your powers, he will have a greater chance of destroying you. He's already tried once, and I believe that the failure of his two assassins to eliminate you will mean that he will move forward his plans for the Ring of Amon in an attempt to distract me and those who work for me long enough so that he can get to you. *You* are the creature he fears most. If he can kill you, he believes that he will be able to carry out his plans unchecked."

"Don't worry, Trey," Tom said. "Lucien and I are not about to let that evil bastard get his talons into you."

Lucien nodded. "We have places where you will be safe and people who can look out for you while you are there. Once we can put an end to his plans regarding the ring, we will find a more permanent solution."

"Why can't I help you and Tom?" Trey asked.

"It's simply too dangerous," Lucien replied, shaking his head. "We need to stop him from using the ring, but you are not sufficiently in control of your powers at this time. I simply cannot allow you to be placed in such jeopardy right now."

"Lucien's right," Tom said. "You'll get your chance to help us in the future, if that is what you want to do. And by God, I hope it is, because you are going to be one huge bloody handful for anybody to cope with, so you are. But right now we need to get you safe and get this ring business sorted out."

Lucien nodded and took a deep breath, everything now settled in his mind. When he next spoke to the Irishman it was in a brisk and businesslike manner.

"Tom, would you please go and ask Alexa to join us? I'd like her to accompany Trey to the safe house." He turned to Trey. "Alexa will remain with you for the duration of your stay. She is an incredibly adept sorceress and will be a great asset to ensuring your safety."

Trey's first reaction was to tell Lucien that he really didn't think he needed a girl to look after him, but, in truth, he was extremely relieved to hear that Alexa was going to be with him if he was forced to go into hiding. He was certain that Lucien would ensure that he and Alexa were well provided for, and as soon as he and Tom had sorted out this matter with the ring, he would send for them again.

"Where are you sending me?" he asked. "And how long do you think I might need to be there?"

Lucien considered the question. "I have a house outside New Jersey. We will arrange for a private jet to take you and Alexa there, where you will be cared for by one of our people. She is completely trustworthy and has been with us for a very long time. She'll also be delighted to have house guests to spoil. I shouldn't think that it will be necessary for you to be there for more than two or three months. Tom or I will visit whenever we are able."

"Are you going to war, Lucien?"

"No," Lucien replied, "not yet. But I fear that the time will come in the not-too-distant future."

18

Tom rushed in, calling for Lucien. The vampire rose to his feet at the same time as Trey, who had been sitting reading on the settee. One look at the scarred Irishman's face was enough to make Trey's stomach roll over sickeningly. He glanced between the vampire and the other man, wondering what could have happened to make Tom look so scared.

"What's happened, Tom?" Lucien asked.

"It's Alexa. She was seen going into the research library to pull up some information on the Ring of Amon," Tom said, his face ashen and etched with concern. "She was keen to look up a particular reference to it in a book on demon lore that we recently acquired. Anyway, one of our people went in there a short while later to see if she wanted a drink. Her research materials, pens, and pad were all neatly laid out on the table, along with a number of books, but Alexa was gone. She went in the door, but never came out."

Trey looked over to Lucien, who was now standing in the center of the room and seemed unable to move.

Tom reached out and handed Lucien a scrap of paper. The message was handwritten in an ornate, flowing style. Trey could see the note as Lucien held it up to read the

180

words neatly penned on its surface. One look at the flowing script, and he instinctively knew that it had been written in blood; the bright red living ink had turned a coppery brown where it had dried on the white paper. The message was simple:

> *If you wish to see Alexa in one piece again,*
> *bring the boy to me.*

Trey could see that the bottom of the note was signed with a large letter *C*. He frowned at the perversity of the small *xo* that had been added after this, as if the note Caliban was sending to his brother was a simple reminder to pick up the shopping or the laundry.

Lucien screwed the paper into his fist and stared ahead into the distance. His eyes blazed with the same ferocity that Trey had witnessed during their session in the squash courts, and the muscles in his jaw worked away at the side of his face as if he was chewing at some invisible piece of food.

"He's got her, hasn't he?" Trey said eventually.

Lucien nodded, but would not meet the boy's eyes.

"Do we know where he has taken her?" Lucien asked.

"Holland," Tom said. "We ran a tracing spell as soon as we found she was gone. They made no effort to try to block it, so they must want us to know exactly where she is and that she is still alive. They're on the move with her, and they look as if they are heading in the direction of Amsterdam. Martin has phoned ahead to get a jet fueled and ready at City Airport. We can leave as soon as you give us the nod, Lucien."

Lucien looked down at the crumpled paper in his hand, his brow creasing as though seeing it for the first time. He looked back at Tom, and gave him a nod. "Tell Martin that we'll be there in thirty minutes. Tom, I want you to call our people in Holland. Get them to ensure that we don't have any trouble getting through quickly at the other end."

"Already done it. We have a man at Schiphol Airport whom we've used before. We won't have any problems there."

The Irishman's eyes were flinty now, and Trey caught a glimpse of the hell-raising, ne'er-do-well youth that he had described himself as.

Lucien was still staring ahead, his mind in overdrive as he considered the options and possible outcomes. Trey could tell from the way he kept furrowing his brow that he did not think any of them were good.

"Do we have a full travel kit ready?" he asked.

"Everything will be downstairs in ten minutes," Tom replied.

"Good. Then we should go." He started to walk out of the room, followed by Tom.

"What about me?" Trey said.

Lucien turned and fixed Trey with a look. "You're not coming, Trey—for all the reasons that we discussed earlier about my brother's intentions as far as you are concerned.

182

Besides, you are not in a fit state to go anywhere right now. I'll have someone come up and take you to the airport and from there you will go on to New Jersey. The plan for you is still the same."

"But the note. It says—"

"I am brutally aware of what the note says, Trey. But do you really think that I am capable of making the trade suggested by my brother? That I will take you there to him so that he can butcher you *and* Alexa in front of me? My brother's soul—if indeed he still has one—might be a moral vacuum, but mine is not. I am not willing to sacrifice one innocent life for another, even if that other is my daughter's. If you believe that I am capable of such a thing, perhaps you are not the person that I thought you to be."

A sudden storm of fury swelled within Trey. He rose up to his full height and met the vampire's stare. "I am not a child, Lucien. You told me that yourself. You can't tell me in one breath that I have to grow up and accept the knowledge of what I have become, and then treat me like a baby in the next."

"Trey, listen—"

"No, *you* listen to me! Recently you asked me to trust you with my life. I had no reason to do so, but something about you and the things you said made me do it. You *saved* my life, Lucien. You repaid my trust in you and I am truly grateful for that. Now I'm asking *you* to trust *me*; trust me with Alexa's life, because if Caliban gets even the slightest idea that you have turned up without me, she's dead. You told me earlier that it's Alexa's spells that have been helping me stay out of Caliban's radar. So if anything happens to her, I'm as good as dead anyway." He swallowed, the noise sounding ridiculously loud in his ears. "So you might as well *use* me to help give Alexa, *and me*, the best chance of getting through this in one piece." He raised his eyebrows questioningly. It was impossible for him to maintain eye contact with the vampire any longer, and a big part of him wanted to back down, bend to the will of that stare, and apologize for his outburst. Instead he looked down at the carpet for respite, before continuing in a smaller voice: "I'll keep out of your way and do exactly what you or Tom tells me to do, but you should take me with you if you want to stand any chance of getting her back."

Lucien stared at him and slowly shook his head.

Tom gave a nervous cough from behind him. "He's got a point, Lucien. If we leave him behind, he's in danger. If we take him with us, he's in danger, but we have it within our power to protect him. And as he says, he might be the only way of getting her back alive. It's his call, Lucien, and you have to respect his right to make it."

Lucien stood there like a great granite statue. Time seemed to stretch out—an invisible elastic, pulling the tension in the room taut along with it. It was time they didn't have, and Trey was aware of this.

Tom leaned in close and said in a low voice, "You've already lost Alexa's mother to that evil creature. Don't lose your daughter too. I'll take responsibility for the boy's well-being and make sure that he is not put in too much danger. And besides," he said, his stony face close to Lucien's, "I seem to remember a certain vampire being held up by the throat and wondering whether he was about to get his face gnawed off by that boy standing over there. He's tough— just like his father, by all accounts. And if it comes to it, I'm sure that he'd be able to fight his way out of a corner."

"He's injured, Tom."

"He's on the mend, Lucien. He heals a hell of a lot faster than you do and, like I said, I'll make sure he's not put in any danger."

At this, Lucien flicked a glance toward Tom before returning his gaze to Trey.

"You are to do everything that Tom tells you to, *without question*. Do you understand?"

Trey nodded in rhythm with his hammering heart. "Thank you, Lucien."

"You might want to reconsider that thank-you once you see what it is we are about to face. Pack some clothes in a rucksack—we're leaving in twenty minutes."

Lucien left in the elevator, leaving Tom alone with Trey. The older man gave him the briefest of smiles and a nod of the head that told Trey everything he needed to know.

"I'm pretty scared, Tom," Trey said, returning the smile.

"Good. Then you'll probably survive," Tom replied. "Now get your arse in gear—we don't have much time."

19

The black BMW pulled out of the garage and sped up the
Aspen Way, heading for the A1020. The giant, hulking shape
of the Canary Wharf building loomed into sight through
Trey's window. Its white warning beacon pulsating at the
tower's apex made him think of the dangers ahead, and
while he had very little idea of what they might face when
they got to Holland, he was sure of one thing: It wasn't going to be pleasant.

A man that Trey hadn't seen around the building before
was driving; Lucien sat beside him in the passenger seat.
Tom and Trey were in the back, Tom tapping at the keyboard of a laptop and barking instructions into a Bluetooth
headset to someone at the airport in Holland.

Tom took a call on his phone. He listened intently to the
person on the other end of the line before thanking them and
ending the call.

"We've found her," Tom said. "They appear to be holding her at a location just outside of the city. She's alive."

Lucien nodded his head, his eyes fixed on the road
ahead.

"We'll have the address in no time. We have everyone
working to keep on top of this situation, Lucien. Caliban's

people are making no attempt to block our attempts to trace her, so if they move her, we'll know about it."

Before they left in the car, Trey had followed Tom downstairs and through the office complex, and finally entered a door set in the wall next to the meeting rooms that Alexa had neglected to point out during her tour of that floor. Trey found himself in a medium-sized room that was dominated by a huge, cage-like structure, its walls and ceiling made of metal mesh through which the contents of the cage could clearly be made out. It was an arsenal. Weapons of every description were arranged in rows of locked gun racks, and Trey stared at the armaments, gadgets, and gizmos arranged within the cage, most of which he hadn't the slightest clue as to what they were or what they might be used for. The door to the cage was open, and a giant of a man filled the void where it should have been. His huge red beard looked as though it had not been trimmed in years, and his hair stuck out from his head in all directions. His eyes were a dull gray, like the sea moments before a storm, and every inch of exposed flesh from his chin downward was covered in intricate and colorful tattoos.

"Hjelldid," Tom said, with a nod of his head in the giant's direction.

"Tom," the man grunted back, handing him a large black backpack and a smaller holdall before grunting something indecipherable and turning his back on them to lock the door again.

Tom quickly checked the contents of the backpack and zipped it up, satisfied. The huge guardian of the armory finished securing the door and turned to hand Tom three passports, each of which was briefly opened to check the details before being placed in the smaller bag.

"Tom, I don't have my passport," Trey said, looking from the holdall to the painted colossus who had stepped nearer now and was towering over him menacingly.

"You do now," Tom replied.

"But—"

"But me no buts, Trey. We don't have time for a discussion about the whys and wherefores of everything right now. You'll have to trust me when I say that everything is sorted. *It's what I do*."

Trey shook his head in bewilderment at the speed that everything was happening around him. His chest had started to ache, and he gingerly felt at the bandages through a gap in his shirt to check that he had not begun to bleed again.

Tom zipped the smaller bag up, and, with a nod to the man, ushered Trey back toward the door.

"Right, young man. Let's be getting a march on, shall we?" He paused a moment, fixing Trey with a look. "I'm normally a great advocate of my dear old ma's belief that 'fools rush in where angels fear to tread,' but we don't have time to fiddle-faddle around right now, so just keep by me at all times. I know that you'll have a million and one questions buzzing around in that head of yours, but I really do not have time to be answering any of them right now, OK?"

Trey nodded his assent and determined to try to simply go along with things as best he could. They turned and walked back through the bustling workplace. Everybody in the office kept looking over the tops of their little alcove walls and nodding their encouragement.

There was a hubbub of worried and anxious voices in the room, and Trey looked at the people as he passed.

Tom glanced at him as if reading his thoughts. "Somebody in here is responsible for this," he said in a low voice so that only Trey could hear. "One of those faces is that of the traitor, and when I find out who it is . . ." He trailed off as they approached the elevator.

The woman that Alexa had identified to him as Ruth when she had shown Trey around the offices was standing by the elevator. She had already pressed the Down button for them, and as they approached, she looked up at Tom with a worried expression. "Good luck," she said. "You and Lucien bring her back safe."

Tom nodded to her as the elevator doors opened up in front of them. He and Trey stepped inside, hitting the button for the garage.

They arrived at City Airport, the car dropping them off with their bags before leaving, having been dismissed by Tom. Lucien had left the car quickly, opening the door and running to the shade provided by the overhang outside the terminal entrance. Wearing his dark glasses, a wide-brimmed black hat, and gloves against the winter sun, he must have appeared like some mad eccentric to the other travelers entering the building, most of whom were openly staring at him and his odd behavior.

During the ride, he'd applied a thick lotion to his face and neck. He turned to Trey when he spotted the boy watching him. "Proactive precaution, really. I'll burn to hell when we get out of the car, but at least this stuff will lessen the effect a little."

They were met by a tall man wearing a blue suit, who nodded at Lucien before following him into the terminal building. It was the first time that Trey could remember ever being at an airport, and it seemed incredibly busy to him. People were walking purposefully in every direction as they made the necessary preparations for their trips—collecting tickets, checking in, or grabbing a few of those last-minute essentials from the airport shops. Blue Suit cut a course directly through the thronging crowds and they bypassed the banks of check-in desks, heading directly toward the departure gates. As they approached, Trey was surprised when they veered off to the right, away from the snaking queue of people and toward a smaller door down from the main gate. Blue Suit held up a pass that hung around his neck on a lanyard to a security guard standing in front of the door, who peered at it intensely before nodding at the party. The guard punched a number into a keypad beside the door and held it open, standing back to let them pass.

On the other side, Blue Suit stood aside, and a smaller man with a moon face and a thin, well-kept mustache stepped forward, offering his hand to Lucien.

"Mr. Charron, a pleasure as always." The man shook Lucien's hand and nodded in Trey and Tom's direction. "Mr. O'Callahan . . . young man . . . if you'd all like to follow me, we can have you on your way as quickly as possible." He indicated an area to their left where two uniformed airport officials were standing next to an X-ray scanning device.

Tom handed the three passports over and placed the backpack and holdall onto the device's conveyor belt. One of the guards gestured for him to step forward and waved a handheld metal detector over him as Tom stood with his arms out by his side. Seeming satisfied, the airport security guard told Tom to step aside, and repeated the process on Trey and Lucien.

Meanwhile his colleague checked the passports, glancing up over the top of the travel documents at each of the three travelers in turn.

Trey's heart hammered in his chest as the guard looked at him. Remembering what Tom had said to him, he lifted his chin and smiled, trying to look like a kid going on a trip with his relatives, before turning to pick up his bag from the other end of the table where it had emerged. The security guard handed the passports back to Tom, nodding his satisfaction to the moon-faced man, who had been hovering beside Lucien throughout the process.

"Excellent. Now, Mr. Charron, if you and your travel

companions would like to step this way?" He led them down a small, brightly lit corridor and into a waiting area with blue sofas and chairs around the edge and a small bar in the center. "Your jet is fueled and ready when you are. If you would like to step through that door over there, one of our people will transport you to your aircraft. Is there anything that I can get you before you leave?" he asked.

"You've been most helpful, thank you," Lucien replied, shaking the man's hand again.

Twenty-five minutes later, Trey was sitting opposite Tom in the cabin of a Learjet 60, hurtling through the air at five hundred miles per hour toward Amsterdam.

20

Their arrival in Schiphol Airport and subsequent transfer were as seamless as the London experience. Schiphol was vast in comparison to the City Airport that they had just left, and Tom had to urge Trey along as he slowed to take in the sights around him. They were met at the airport by Tom's contact, Jens van der Zande, who showed them to a large black Mercedes that was waiting at the front of the departure building. As soon as they were all safely inside, the car sped away toward the city, Jens driving expertly through the taxis and other cars that were leaving the airport grounds at the same time.

For Trey, who had never been farther than France on a day trip with the care-home staff, the whole trip seemed utterly surreal. Only a few hours earlier he'd been drinking tea with Tom and Lucien in the apartment in London, and now here he was speeding along a motorway in Holland, watching the flat arable landscape flash past his window.

"I'd like to thank you for arranging everything at such short notice, Jens. It couldn't have been very easy," Lucien said.

"Not a problem, Lucien. We had to pull in a few favors

with some people, but they were all very willing to help us when they heard the circumstances."

"Where are we booked in?"

"The Amstel InterContinental. I booked two suites, as specified by Tom: one for you and the other for Tom and the boy."

Jens glanced at Trey in the rearview mirror and gave him a slight nod of the head.

"Jens, did you get the things that I asked for?" Tom said, leaning forward in his seat.

"The grenades and the MP5K are all in a bag in the trunk. We had some trouble with the shotgun that you specified, but I think that you'll be relatively satisfied with the alternative model that we have obtained."

Tom winked at Trey, who was staring at him in disbelief. "There's no need to fear the wind if your haystacks are tied down," he said with a grin.

"Have we been able to ascertain if they have moved my daughter?" Lucien asked.

"Our sources would indicate that she is still in the same building that they took her to at the start. We are running trace spells every ten minutes or so, and Alexa's captors seem perfectly happy for them to succeed. They're making absolutely no attempt to hide her, Lucien. She's alive, but we have been unable to ascertain if she has been harmed in any way."

The inside of the car went silent as each of them considered this response. There was nothing more to be said, so they remained quiet for the rest of the journey, the quiet rumble of the tires as they rolled along the tarmac surface of the road the only accompaniment to their thoughts. The countryside outside began to change as they exited the motorway, the sudden appearance of shops and residences signaling the outskirts of the city, before the space between the buildings became less and less and then seemed to disappear entirely, consumed by the claustrophobic metropolis of the city center. Trey sat staring at the scenery flashing past him and wished that his first visit to Amsterdam was under happier circumstances so that he could stop and take in some of the sights that he glimpsed as they sped by.

"Here we are," Jens said, pulling up in front of the hotel. On their right, the Amstel River sluggishly made its way through the city. Barges and houseboats stretched along the banks on either side of the coffee-colored water.

"Tom and Trey will get checked in," Lucien said. He turned in his seat to face the two of them. "You'll want to prepare your things, Tom. Jens and I will go ahead and take a look at the area around where Alexa is being held. Is that OK, Jens?"

"Of course, Lucien. There are some things that I wanted to discuss with you anyway. We can do it in the car on the way."

"Be careful, guys," Tom said as he got out of the car. "They'll be watching for you."

Jens popped the trunk from inside the car, and Trey and Tom were able to retrieve their bags. Tom removed his

195

backpack, then hefted a long black canvas holdall from deep within the trunk and hoisted it onto his shoulder, winking at Trey as he did so.

Trey followed him up the stairs leading to the hotel entrance, turning at the top to watch as the car sped away.

The lobby of the hotel was a vast, brightly lit open space, dominated by a huge mahogany staircase that led to a balcony running around the entire room. An enormous chandelier hung down over the staircase, its light reflected back up from the highly polished black-and-white marble floor tiles.

Trey had never been in a building that reeked of opulence as much as this one did, and he stood inside the entrance door gawking up at the grandeur all around him until Tom gently took him by the elbow and steered him toward the reception desk.

The receptionist was a tall man in rimless spectacles that reflected the computer screen that he was peering at as they approached. He stopped typing on his keyboard and smiled up at them.

"Can I help you, gentlemen?" he asked. Trey could hardly detect a trace of an accent in his perfect English.

"Mr. O'Callahan. I believe that you have a suite reserved in my name?"

The receptionist returned to his keyboard and, after a brief pause, checked them in and issued them their room card. He pressed a button to summon the porter, and while they were waiting, Trey looked around again at the cavernous surroundings. He peered across at the concierge, who was standing behind another desk a short distance away and was dressed in the same uniform as the receptionist. The man wore a far-from-genuine smile on his face as he waited for two American tourists to finish their argument about which particular trip they wanted to go on that evening, and Trey got the impression that they had been there for some time. Sensing that he was being watched, the man glanced over in Trey's direction and gave him a polite nod.

The porter turned up, and the hunched little man insisted on putting their bags on a giant metal trolley before escorting them to their rooms. He took Trey's holdall and placed it on the base next to Tom's, but was waved away by the Irishman as he reached for the long canvas bag hanging over his shoulder. "That's grand, thank you," Tom said, "but I'll carry this one up myself."

They followed the porter over to the polished wooden doors of the elevator and up to their rooms.

21

"I can't believe that you tipped him twenty euros!" Trey said as soon as the porter had left them and closed the door. "Bloody hell, all he did was wheel that trolley up here with our bags on it, and you go and give him twenty euros. I'd have pushed that thing up here for ten!"

He looked around him at the room. He'd expected a nice room—he doubted if they had anything but nice rooms in a place like this—but the suite that they were booked into was lush. Trey moved from the seating area into the main bedroom, where an enormous four-poster bed dominated the space.

"Tom, this place is huge."

"Yeah? Well, you go and have a little explore, Trey. I've got a few things that I need to sort out right now."

Trey walked through the bedroom and into the immense bathroom that came off it. He helped himself to the shampoos and soaps that were arranged neatly around the shelf above the sink, and tried on one of the thick, fluffy bathrobes that were hanging behind the door—putting it on over his clothes.

"Slight problem, Tom—double bed only," Trey shouted through.

"That'll be yours, then. I'll be on the sofa out here," Tom

replied, adding under his breath, "not that you or I will be getting any sleep for the next day or so."

Trey threw himself back onto the bed, popping one of the chocolate squares that had been set on the pillows into his mouth, and tried to wrap his head around the day so far. He looked up at the lined roof of the four-poster and frowned, the sweet chocolate suddenly tasting bitter in his mouth as his thoughts turned to Alexa and where she might be right now. He rolled out of the bed and walked slowly back into the living area.

Tom was kneeling on the floor, laying out the considerable arsenal that he had unpacked from the bag taken from the back of Jens's car. Trey stepped close and looked at the collection.

"That looks like some awesome hardware, Tom."

The Irishman looked up, his face serious as he indicated the weapons arranged in front of him. "Don't you get any ideas about touching any of this kit now, Trey. I'm scared silly handling some of this stuff, and I know what I'm doing. The last thing any of us needs right now is you shooting your foot off or something."

He started to strip the small machine gun, laying the pieces methodically on a square of white material that he had placed to one side.

"What's that? An Uzi?" Trey asked.

"No," Tom said, without looking up, concentrating on his task. "Heckler & Koch MP5K submachine gun. Savage tool. Great stopping power."

"What are they?" Trey said, pointing with his foot at a line of six cylindrical canisters.

"Concussion grenades. Just about the best little beasties you can use in enclosed spaces that you want cleared of anything alive before you enter. My experience in dealing with nether-creatures in the past has led me to believe that 'when in doubt, blow the thing to oblivion' is a good mantra to stay alive by.

"This," he said, holding up an ugly-looking weapon, "is a Remington 870 Modular Combat Shotgun—not my weapon of choice, but it would seem that they had trouble getting a Mossberg in time. The rest of it is just bits and bobs that might or might not come in handy." He looked up at the boy and noted the confused look on his face. "None of this stuff is particularly useful for *killing* nether-creatures like vampires. But even a vampire goes over when hit full on with a couple of rounds from this beast," he said, patting the stock of the weapon. "Then it's a matter of dispatching them in the most appropriate manner." He nodded toward the bag, and Trey noticed the pile of sharpened wooden stakes in the bottom.

"Do they work?" he asked.

"Supposed to. If you survive long enough to get a chance to use one. And you manage to hit the heart. Other than that, it's beheading, fire, explosives, or entombment. The options aren't great."

"What about a crossbow? Like you see in the movies?"

Tom smiled at him. "Have you ever tried firing one of

those things?" he said, with a shake of his head. "No. I think the hand method is about the only way to be sure."

Trey paused, uncertain whether or not to ask the question that had been nagging at him since he had first seen the note left for Lucien. "You don't think Caliban has any intention of returning Alexa, do you? Regardless of what Lucien does or doesn't do."

Tom looked up at him and inhaled sharply through his nose. He held the breath for a couple of seconds before letting it out again. "No. I think there's more chance of Lucien getting an audience with the Pope. Caliban is using Alexa to lure Lucien in so that he can eliminate him. He knows that Lucien can't stand by and let him use the Ring of Amon, so he'll try to remove him from the equation. It's a good tactic, and if it works, he'll be free to turn this world into hell."

"What's Lucien doing with Jens?"

"He's recceing the site where Caliban is holding Alexa and then he'll be back with a report on how we should approach. Jens could undoubtedly have told us everything that we will need to know, but Lucien will want to be doing something—anything—to keep his mind off what might happen to Alexa now that his brother has got hold of her."

"Tom, how *did* Caliban manage to get to Alexa? If he's as intent on eliminating Lucien as you say he is, I'd have thought that the building in London would have been more secure."

"More secure? That place is bullet- and bombproof, has security systems coming out of its arse and a team of people that weave enough witchcraft in and out of it to make your head go pop." He stopped and put the magazine he had been loading with ammunition down. "It's the question that Lucien and I have been asking ourselves since she was taken."

"Could it have been Hopper?" Trey asked.

"No, he'd already gone by then. Although that treacherous, vile vermin had a big hand in the attack on you. He's unquestionably working for Caliban now, but my guess is that he was charged with spying on you and feeding back any information that he could. Besides, he's a cowardly worm and wouldn't have had the guts for something like this. No," he continued, "I think that as much as it pains me to admit it, Alexa was taken by someone inside our own organization. There's a rat in the camp, Trey, and as soon as this nonsense is over with, I'm going to find out who it is and permanently separate them from their oxygen supply."

The stomach-gripping reality of the whole situation snapped into clearer focus for Trey. He turned from Tom and looked through the window at the river below, playing out each scenario in his head. However many times he rewound and edited the scenes in his mind's eye, they never finished with a happy ending.

"So Lucien is going to try to rescue Alexa alone?" Trey asked.

"Not quite alone—he'll have me and Messrs. Heckler and

Koch with him," Tom replied, patting the submachine gun that he had reassembled.

"And me. I'm coming too," Trey said.

"Ah, no. We brought you because it was safer to have you with us right now than to have you on your own—what with there being a security problem back in London. But there is not a snowball in hell's chance of you coming with Lucien and me up against Caliban. Uh-uh." Tom shook his head and started to get up.

"I don't really have any choice, Tom. If Caliban succeeds in destroying you all, I'm as good as dead. At least if I come with you, I'll have a fighting chance and might be of some use." Trey turned from the window and fixed Tom with a hard look. "You've seen how strong and quick I am—*surely* Lucien would rather have me there helping than sitting here waiting for Caliban's goons to come and pick me off. Besides, you've just told me that all of these guns and stuff aren't going to be of any real use against Caliban. You need nether-creatures to fight him and his kind."

Tom packed the arms back into the canvas bag and pulled the zipper shut. He got up and looked at Trey, a worried frown cresting his features.

"That's not my call to make, Trey," he said. "What you say makes perfect sense, and if it were up to me, I think I'd like you around to help. But you're only a young lad and Lucien feels very protective toward you. I can't see him allowing you to get involved with all this. The dangers are too great."

Just then a piercing klaxon went off. The deafening noise came from the alarm bell above the door and it filled the confines of the room, making both of them hunch their shoulders and look about in dread.

"It's the fire alarm," Trey shouted over the din, moving toward the door.

"Wait!" Tom ordered and held up a warning hand to the teenager. He moved to the windows and looked out at the street below. Stepping into the center of the room again, he unzipped the bag and removed a handgun, a Glock 17. Throwing the bag over his shoulder, he gestured for Trey to step away from the door.

Tom pulled the door open an inch or two, his right hand holding the gun out of sight by his side, and peered out as other guests hurried along the corridor toward the emergency exits. He noted the concern on the faces of the people as they moved along the passageway, and how they were moving quickly but in an orderly way. Some were supporting older relatives who were less able-bodied than themselves.

A piercing scream from a woman toward the rear of the group filled the confined space of the hotel corridor, and that noise changed the makeup of the scene in the time it took to issue it from her mouth. Guests glanced behind them, then rushed forward, pushing at the people in front of them to get away from whatever it was that they had seen.

Tom moved slightly to his right, still keeping the partially closed door between him and the unfolding drama

204

outside. He craned his neck to get a look at what it was that the woman had seen to make her let out that horrible shriek, and at the rear of the group just behind the screaming woman he spied the source of the panic.

The concierge, whom only a short while ago they had watched helping the American couple downstairs, was loping up the corridor toward the fleeing guests, a ten-inch kitchen knife held up in his fist. One look at the man's face told Tom that he was intent on using the savage-looking blade, and he quickly raised the gun that he had been holding at his side, glancing momentarily over his shoulder to check that Trey was still safely away from the door, unable to see the horror that was unfolding.

The concierge grabbed the woman by the hair and her scream reverberated around the walls of the corridor. Tom aimed the gun, drawing a bead on the man's chest, and was about to fire when another guest ran into his line of sight and pandemonium broke out in the small corridor. People were running in every direction: a stampede of human panic that obscured Tom's view of the concierge and his hapless victim.

Everyone was frantically making their way to the emergency exit now, desperate to find another route to freedom that wasn't blocked by the murderous staff member. They tore and pulled at each other, frantic to get out at any cost.

As the crowd surged ahead of him, Tom saw the concierge stand up and smooth his hair back across his head. His eyes were black glass marbles—like the dead eyes of a porcelain doll—and his mouth broke into a sick grin as he ran past the door and into the back of the gaggle of screaming people clambering for the exit. It was impossible for Tom to get a shot off without risking killing one of the people himself. He quickly turned his head away from the scene and beckoned Trey toward him, a look of utter revulsion on his face.

"I think Caliban's experiment has begun. He's used the Ring of Amon on some of the people here at the hotel. He must have discovered we were staying here. There's nothing we can do. They've gone mad. We have to leave. Now."

Trey nodded and moved to the man's side. Tom opened the door, wide enough to put his head outside and, after a quick glance, pulled it fully open and looked out into the corridor.

The crowd at the packed exit was still clawing at the door, trying to escape. A body—that of an elderly man—lay on the floor, a rapidly widening pillow of blood spreading out onto the carpet beneath his head. Two men were bravely trying to wrestle the knife out of the maniac's hands.

Tom stepped out and strode purposefully toward the three men. He pistol-whipped the concierge around the temple, the metal handgun making a dull *thunk* as it connected with the man's skull. Before the man had even hit the floor, Tom had turned away and moved back in Trey's direction. Moving swiftly past him, he grabbed the stunned boy by the shoulder and propelled him up the corridor, in the opposite direction to the emergency exit door, the shouts and screams of the hotel guests ringing in their ears as they left the scene.

Trey's stomach lurched at the sight of a dead woman lying on the floor no more than twelve feet from their own room door. The acid taste of vomit filled his mouth and he had to struggle not to retch. Tom grabbed him by the arm and pulled him behind him, stepping over the prone corpse.

"That woman—" Trey said.

"Dead. Nothing we can do for her, Trey. You can say a prayer for her later if that's what floats your boat, but right now we have to get out of here."

Tom dragged the boy to the elevators, stabbing repeatedly at the button to call them.

"Tom, we can't take the elevators. The fire alarm's ringing."

"This is not a fire, Trey, not yet anyway. And this lift is the quickest and safest way down right now." He pressed the button, readying the gun as the elevator doors opened.

As they reached the lobby, the doors slid apart to reveal another scene of mayhem. People with panic-stricken eyes were pushing for the front door as others grabbed at them, peeling them away in an attempt to make their own escape. An older woman had fallen down the staircase, and a young man—possibly her son—was holding her gray-haired head in his lap, pleading for someone to help. Tom took one look at the scene, weighed up his options, and, grabbing Trey by the arm, headed off to his left toward a sign pointing to the swimming pool and gymnasium. He kicked open the door in front of him and raced down the corridor. The strong disinfectant tang of the pool's chlorine carried on the air from somewhere up ahead.

The fear that Trey had been feeling began to build again, his head swimming with the sights and sounds that assaulted him from every direction.

"Tom, where are we going?"

"Just keep up," Tom insisted.

"But—"

Trey stopped as a strangled scream cut into the air behind him. He turned to see the receptionist, who had welcomed them with kind smiles only an hour before, flying at him aiming a metal-and-wood bar stool at his head, his glistening black eyes set into a mask of rage.

Tom turned in time to see the arc of the chair and started to reach for his gun, knowing that he would be too late to stop the wooden seat from crushing the boy's skull.

He never even got a chance to click off the weapon's safety catch.

One moment the chair was hurtling toward Trey's head. The next it thudded into the great barrel chest of the were-monster that towered over his assailant. Trey swatted the chair aside and roared at the man, flecks of spittle landing on the receptionist's glasses as he stared into Trey's huge mouth. Trey pushed the man backward in a

208

defensive gesture—to Tom it appeared no more than a swift shove—and the receptionist smashed into the corridor wall, pieces of plasterboard raining down onto his unconscious body.

The same feeling of power that he had experienced during his fight with Lucien coursed through every part of him again. Except this time he had even more control. A tiny part of him urged him to attack the man now that he was down—to rend and tear with tooth and claw. But he dialed out these thoughts as quickly as they appeared, recognizing them as some animalistic throwback to the uncontrolled Wolfan state. Instead he leaned forward, checking that the man was still breathing regularly and hoping that he was not too badly hurt.

"He'll be OK," Tom said from behind him, and Trey turned to face the Irishman, who gestured over his shoulder and set off back down the corridor at a run.

Trey took one last look at the receptionist before setting off after his friend, silently padding along with a long, effortless gait, his ears brushing against the ceiling despite his hunching forward in an effort to make himself less tall. At one point Tom had looked over his shoulder to check that he was still behind him, and Trey noted the look of horror that flashed across the other man's face as he caught sight of the giant lycanthrope hot on his heels.

Before he reached the entrance to the pool, Tom grabbed one of the towels from a row of shelves on which they were stacked in neatly folded bundles. He threw the cotton bathsheet behind him, smiling as it snagged an outstretched claw.

"To cover your modesty when we get outside. Now, move it," he said, opening the double doors at the end of the passage. "There's no telling how many more of those lunatics are around."

They entered the foyer to the health suite and stopped as a chirruping sound came from Tom's trouser pocket. He hooked his mobile out and held it to his ear.

". . . No, we're fine, Lucien . . . yes, he's used the ring and all hell broke loose . . . No, we're coming out via an exit near the rear, I'm trying to locate an emergency door near the pool . . . Yes, Lucien, Trey's fine. You might want to see if you can get him a jacket and some trousers to put on, though . . . that's right . . . no, it was unavoidable—he was attacked, but he was poetry in motion, you should have seen him."

Tom listened to Lucien for a short while more. "Right, we'll see you there," he said, and pressed the button to end the call.

He turned and smiled nervously at the sight of Trey standing next to him. "C'mon, White Fang, let's get going. Lucien is meeting us with a car round the back."

22

Trey morphed back just before they emerged from behind the building, wrapping the towel around his waist and running across the street to the waiting car that was parked with its doors open and the engine running. As they sped off in the direction of Dam Square, Tom filled Lucien in on what had happened at the hotel.

Lucien sat and listened impassively, never interrupting Tom until he got to the part where Trey had morphed to defend himself against the attack from the lunatic receptionist.

"Was the man seriously hurt?" Lucien asked.

"No. He may have a break here or there, and he'll have a doozy of a headache when he comes round, but he's alive, if that's what you mean," Tom said, looking over at Trey reassuringly and offering him a little wink.

"They went insane," Trey said into the silence that followed. "Those men just went mad. There was nothing in their eyes, just a blackness. And that poor woman that was murdered . . ."

"Those men were not to blame for their actions, Trey," Lucien said. "The Ring of Amon will make killers out of anyone who hears the wearer recite the Spell of the Dead.

Our only hope is to get to Caliban before he can do any further damage. As we feared, the ring's power is effective over the mobile networks, so it will not be long before he scales up the test and affects hundreds, if not thousands, of people."

The silence descended on them again as the occupants considered what had happened. The hum of the car's tires on the road was regularly punctuated by the quick *clock-clock* sound made whenever they went over one of the city's numerous tram rails. Trey looked out of the window at the people who walked by the canals or sat in the last of the day's winter sunshine, enjoying a coffee outside one of the roadside cafés. He thought how bizarre it was that they had no idea what was happening in their beautiful city, and how all this would change in an instant if Caliban were allowed to unleash the dreadful power of the ring on its inhabitants.

"Jens and I have been to look at the building that they are holding Alexa in. There's no easy way in for us, Tom. It's an old unused factory on the edge of the city. Because of its situation there's no way to approach it without being detected, so our options are severely limited. I think that our only choice will be a frontal assault. Jens will gather some men together to provide us with plenty of cover, but we'll have to take our chances going in."

They slowed down and stopped at a traffic light, watching as the cars and bicycles streamed by in front of them.

"I think we might be missing the bigger picture here, Lucien," Tom said quietly. He shifted in his seat slightly so that he could see Lucien's eyes in the rearview mirror. "Why would he bring you all the way here and set all of this up if he wanted to kill you before you got into that building? You've already said that he's making no attempt to stop us from locating Alexa. He *wants* us to come to him. That little show he put on for us at the hotel just now was nothing more than muscle flexing. He wants you to know that he can unleash that power when he chooses. He wants you to try to stop him. He's drawing you in, Lucien. And if that is the case, a frontal assault of the kind you have just described may be counterproductive to what we hope to achieve. Hell, it could be disastrous."

The car started to pull away again, speeding up through the intersection and heading out of the center of the town. Lucien turned around in his seat to look at Tom, his face pinched as he weighed up what the Irishman had just said. Then, to Trey's complete surprise, he turned in his direction and raised his eyebrows. "And what do you think, Trey? Everyone seems to have an opinion on how I should try to get my daughter back safely, so what's yours, eh?" His voice was harsh and strained, and Trey felt himself pull back slightly. Trey thought that he had never seen Lucien look as vulnerable as he did in those moments. He looked down at his feet and avoided the vampire's stare. There was nothing that he could say that would help, so he simply held his tongue.

Tom shifted uncomfortably in his seat.

Lucien sighed, and when Trey glanced up again the

vampire's expression had changed to one of sorrow and regret. "I'm sorry, Trey, I had no right to talk to you like that. It was unacceptable. Please accept my apologies."

Trey held Lucien's eyes for a moment. "I think that Tom is correct in how he sees the whole thing," he said quietly. "Your brother is using Alexa to get to you. The rest is just smoke and mirrors. He knew you'd come, and my guess is that he didn't really expect you to follow his instructions and bring me along and that he probably doesn't care whether you did or not. *You're* the one he really wants, Lucien. If he eliminates you, he can carry out his plans for the Ring of Amon and deal with the rest of us at his leisure."

Lucien nodded slowly before turning back around to stare at the road ahead through the windshield. He took a deep breath, inhaling slowly through his nose and tilting his head back until it stopped against the headrest behind him.

"You're both right, of course. My desire to rescue Alexa appears to have clouded my judgment somewhat. Thank you both for showing a very old vampire the error of his thinking." His mood shifted, and when he spoke next, there was a resolution and determination in his voice that was good to hear again. "If my brother wants me to go to him, I will. As soon as the sun goes down, I shall go and see what he has in store for me and bring Alexa home again."

"We'll go in together, Lucien, we'll show Caliban just what—"

"I'm going alone, Thomas. It's too dangerous."

214

"Like hell you are," Tom growled from the backseat. "If you think that I am going to let you go into that butcher's lair on your own, you've got another think coming. It's a trap, Lucien, and even if your brother is making no attempt to conceal that fact, it's still a trap. I'm coming along, and there is nothing you can do short of killing me yourself that is going to stop me!"

"OK, Tom. Thank you. I'd appreciate your help and your counsel. We'll go in together."

"I'm coming too," Trey said, staring down into the footwell and trying not to allow his fear and anxiety to show up in his voice.

"Absolutely not, I forbid it," Lucien replied, his jaw set determinedly.

"Damn it, Lucien!" Trey's angry voice filled the cabin of the car. "You're not my father!"

"No, I am not. But when he was killed, I resolved to fulfill my promise to him that I would ensure that his son would be kept safe. I certainly have no intention of allowing you to face your father's murderer and suffer the same fate." He paused, adding, "I knew it was a mistake to bring you along. Do not make this any more difficult than it already is, Trey."

"I want to help, Lucien."

"Then help by doing as I ask and staying out of this."

Lucien looked out of the window as if to emphasize that this was the end of the matter. Trey followed his gaze and watched the tall gabled buildings flash past and the

215

people going about their everyday business. He thought of the woman lying dead in a pool of her own blood outside the hotel room. She would not have expected to die that day. She might have had plans to go to the museum or take a trip on one of the riverboats that ferried tourists through the canal system. She was someone's daughter and possibly someone's mother, and now those people would never see her alive again. For the first time in years, his thoughts turned to his own mother. He struggled to conjure up the picture of her face—he had pushed all thoughts of his parents out of his mind for such a long time—but all he could remember was her smile and her kind blue eyes, framed by long brown hair. If he was honest, even these memories were from the pictures of her that his grandmother had shown him.

"How did my mother die?" he asked.

"Trey, I really do not think that this is a good time for me to—"

"*How did she die, Lucien?*"

Lucien continued to stare out of his window, not turning to face the boy in the back. "Your mother and father had kept your birth a secret for such a long time. They moved around constantly to avoid being detected, and they were extremely careful to cover any signs and signals that might give away their *true nature*. Your father and I had stopped working together, but something came up, and I needed his help. We had to travel together to Italy," he said in a low voice. "It was during the time that you and your parents were living in France, in a small farmhouse."

Trey cast his mind back but recalled very little about the house except for the kitchen, which he remembered as a large open space that was always warm and smelled of the herbs that his mother dried in little bundles from a wooden beam in the center of the room.

"Caliban and two of his minions managed to gain entry to the farmhouse—despite the protections that your father and I had placed upon it. Their initial intention was to steal you away and use you as a bargaining chip to stop your father and me from carrying out any further activities against them. Ultimately, they wanted you dead.

"Luckily, your mother was alerted to their presence and managed to wake the au pair who slept in the room adjoining yours. It was nothing short of a miracle that the girl managed to smuggle you out of the house without being caught, and it is thanks to her and the bravery of your mother that you are alive today. Your mother confronted my brother and tried to buy you and the girl more time to escape by telling him that she had hidden you somewhere in the house, somewhere that they would never find you. Caliban and the two demons that accompanied him tore the farmhouse apart in their attempt to locate you. When that proved fruitless, they tore your mother apart as well. They tortured her in an effort to make her tell them where you were, but she never revealed to them who you were with or how you had escaped them."

Trey blinked back the tears that welled up in his eyes, and stared out of the window, taking all of this in.

"I'm coming with you, Lucien," he said, his words causing small clouds of condensation to form on the window that he was staring out of. "Alexa is in trouble—the same kind of trouble that my mother was in. My father couldn't help then, but I can help now. You have to give me a chance to do this. Lucien."

"Stop the car please, Jens," Lucien insisted.

The car pulled in by a curbside. A black wrought-iron handrail separated the pavement from the canal on the other side, and tourists stared into the vehicle that had blocked their path, forcing them up against the rail in order to pass it.

"Jens, please remove Mr. Laporte from the car," Lucien said coldly.

"You can try and dump me here if you like and go on ahead without me, Lucien," Trey said. "I really have no idea how far and how fast I can run as a werewolf, but I'm guessing that I can keep up with this thing easily, even if you get out onto a motorway. So if you want to kick me out right here, go ahead. I'll simply morph into a bloody great wolf in front of all these people and follow you on foot. I imagine that should make a great little lead item on the evening news. Like I said earlier: If you fail, I'm as good as dead anyway. Let me help, Lucien, please."

Lucien stopped Jens with a touch of his hand and the Dutchman sat back down in his seat. Tom fiddled with the zipper of his bag as the uncomfortable silence engulfed them all. The only sound that disturbed the quiet inside the small space was the ticking of the indicator on the dashboard console.

Lucien sighed and turned in his seat to fix the boy with an icy stare. Trey looked back at him, blinking against the intensity of the vampire's gaze.

"Once again, you will stick with Tom at all times and do *exactly* what he tells you to. You are not to do *anything* without his specific say-so. Do I make myself clear?"

"Yes, Lucien."

"I'm only allowing you to come because, beyond weighing you down with chains and throwing you into that canal there, I don't know what the hell else to do with you."

"Thank you, Lucien."

Lucien nodded his head, and Jens pulled the car back onto the road. They continued up the same road before turning at a sign indicating the direction of the highway. The road was full of the cars of people returning home at the end of their working day. Grim expressions were on the faces of the drivers as they battled against the traffic in order to get home to their families as quickly as possible.

Trey sat in the back of the Mercedes and stared out at the lines of cars around them. He thought about his mother and father—memories of them came pouring back to him, memories that he had long since banished into a dark corner of his mind. Great tears slid down his cheeks and he made no attempt to stop them as he had done in the past. He let them fall into his lap, completely surrendering to the weight of the sadness that pressed down upon him.

The other occupants of the car sat quietly, looking anywhere but at the crying boy, allowing the young man to grieve.

They only stopped once during their headlong rush to meet the creature that was hoping to lure them to their deaths. Jens pulled into a small turnoff at Lucien's request, and the vampire jumped out of the car and retrieved something from the trunk.

Tom leaned across the seat during this brief interruption, gesturing with his head toward Lucien as he stood outside. "Evening fix time," he explained in a conspiratorial tone, making a drinking gesture with his hand.

The sun had finally disappeared behind the horizon now, and when Lucien climbed back into the car, he no longer needed the hat and gloves that he had worn throughout the day. Trey watched him as he approached the car. He looked *different* now: He seemed to crackle with that same intensity that Trey had witnessed during their training session together.

Sundown is his time, thought Trey. *Heaven help anything that tries to get in his way now.* Lucien was in his seat and they pulled out and continued their journey again, merging with the last of the early-evening commuters on the road.

"Jens will drive us to the bottom of the road leading to the warehouse," the vampire explained. "He will wait for our signal. If, and when, we escape with Alexa, we will make straight for the airport. Jens will organize the clean-up operation at this end. Tom, do you have the two-way radios?"

Tom dug into his bag and handed one each to Jens and Lucien. He hooked a third to the jerkin that he was wearing.

"Don't I get one?" Trey asked.

"No," said Tom. "D'ya think that I want the sounds of a bloody great werewolf growling and barking down the radio at me?" He turned back to Lucien. "Lucien, I know everything that we said earlier, but are we seriously going to just walk in the front door?"

"Yes. We'll naturally be as cautious as possible, but I don't think that we'll be in any danger until we are all inside the factory itself. Caliban will want us all in one place at the same time so that he can deal with us en masse. He has Alexa, so he knows that you and I will come. Trey is an added bonus—the icing on the cake, as it were."

"Wouldn't we be better waiting until the backup arrives? Just in case anything goes wrong. If we needed help, we'd be able to get it quickly that way."

"If we had more time, and Caliban did not have the Ring of Amon, then that would be my choice too. But we simply do not have that luxury, Tom. We have to do it like this."

"Jeez, it's going to be like the bleedin' gunfight at the O.K. Corral."

"It's not far now, Lucien," Jens said as they came to the

bottom of the exit ramp. "My people will be here shortly. If you wanted to wait for them—"

"No. Thank you, Jens, but we'll be fine. Tell your people to wait. If we need you, we will contact you."

Lucien turned to look at Trey. "As soon as we get out of the car, I want you to morph. I want you to stay in your werewolf form until this is all over and done. On no account should you return back to your human form until we are out of that building with Alexa safely in our hands again. You should be safe if you stay with Tom, but if anything happens to him, I want you to get out of there and get to safety as quickly as possible. As soon as we have located Alexa, you and Tom are to leave with her. Don't wait for me. I must deal with my brother and try to retrieve the ring. Tom, signal Jens, and all of you get to the airport as swiftly as you can and return to London. I repeat—*do not wait for me.*"

Tom glanced over at Trey, an unreadable look on his face as he slowly shook his head. "Doc Holliday and the O.K. bleedin' Corral," he whispered, before leaning forward in his seat to look out of the front of the car as their destination appeared up ahead.

23

The car's tires ground against the loose gravel at the bottom of the road as the car came to a halt, a small cloud of fine dust flowering up into the surrounding air before dispersing on the light breeze. It was getting much darker now, and they could just make out the outline of the factory building in the distance as they got out of the car.

Tom opened the trunk and placed the grenades and ammunition clips in the various pockets, loops, and straps of the sleeveless jerkin that he had on, slinging the shotgun over his back. Picking up the submachine gun, he made sure that the weapon was ready for use, going through the checks as though they were second nature to him. When he finally looked up, he saw Lucien and the werewolf looming over him. A crooked smile played on his lips as he looked at Trey. "Jeez, you are a scary-looking beast, Trey Laporte, so you are."

He hoped that the snarl from the giant man-wolf was a friendly acknowledgment.

"Ready?" Lucien asked.

Trey followed the two older men as they started toward the building. Layers of smells and sounds assaulted his senses from all around and he felt the same dizziness that he had encountered when he had first morphed in front of Lucien. He concentrated, and found that he was able to screen out most of the white noise and quickly regain his equilibrium. As he took in the myriad of smells, he thought that he could detect the faint scent of Alexa in the air, and the thought that she had been dragged to this desolate place against her will caused the hackles on the back of his neck to rise and a low rumbling growl to issue from deep inside his barrel chest.

His eyes flicked toward the sky and the stars, and something stirred within him—a deep and powerful feeling that he had not experienced before suddenly flooding through him. On the previous occasions that he had transformed he had always been inside, but now he was outside, he was filled with such a bewildering sense of *rightness* that he had to fight back the sudden urge to throw back his great wolf head and howl in joy at the euphoria of it all. He had told Alexa that he had felt *alive* in his werewolf state, but this feeling was amplified a hundredfold now. It was as if *this* was where he was truly meant to be: a wolf outside with the wind and the grass and the night sky open above him.

A small cough from Tom brought him out of his reverie, and he forced himself to push these strange thoughts aside and to concentrate again on the task in hand.

The building was about fifty meters away and in complete darkness, but his wolf eyes could pick out the tiniest details of the brickwork around the door, with the broken sign saying "Mittendorf" hanging above it, as though he were viewing it all through high-powered night goggles.

Whoever the Mittendorfs were, they had not used this place in a long time.

Weeds grew up in the wasteland surrounding the building, and most of the windows were either boarded up or smashed from the overexuberant attention of the local youth, who had no doubt attacked the place when drunk on the contents of the empty bottles and cans that lay all around.

Trey scanned the windows and thought that he could detect movement behind some of them, as though people were looking out at their approach while trying to stay hidden. He scanned the windows again, but there was nothing solid to fix upon—the figures behind those broken panes were mere *suggestions* of the things that were really there, and he gave up, sure that he would come to realize what they were soon enough.

They were no more than ten meters from the entrance when two small lights suddenly went on on either side of the open door, their smutty glass shades giving the bulbs beneath a yellow hue so that they looked like jaundiced eyes opening, peering out at them from the grim countenance that was the building's face.

"I don't like this one bit," Tom said in a low voice, flicking the safety switch up on the gun.

Lucien walked on slightly ahead. His step was so light it

hardly disturbed the tiny stones coughed up by the broken asphalt that had once been the path to this place.

They paused in front of the open door, surveying the dark interior. A corridor led away from the entrance, ending in a set of stairs at the rear of the building, and a series of doors led off from either side of the passageway, the rooms behind them dark and foreboding.

"Oh great, a bloody rabbit warren," Tom groaned. "We'd need a full assault team to do this properly. This is madness, Lucien—"

Lucien held up a hand for him to stop. He closed his eyes and stood motionless for a moment, and everything ceased. It was that pure *stop* that Trey had experienced back at the care home just when he had first met Lucien, as though the world had momentarily ceased spinning and everything in it held its breath and waited for it to start again.

Then suddenly it did. Trey blinked as the cacophony of sounds that had filled the night before Lucien had gone into his trance-like state suddenly assaulted his ears again, and he looked over at Tom, who simply shrugged his shoulders at him, a don't-ask-me expression on his face.

"He has Alexa on the second floor," Lucien said, and walked in through the door.

The rooms on this floor had once housed office workers, but they were now merely empty shells. The remains of the furniture had been smashed or set on fire by the vandals. A rusting metal filing cabinet sat in one corner, its bottom drawer jutting out like a child sulking at the mistreatment that it had had to endure.

The factory smelled of decay and neglect. To Trey, it appeared as a brown-and-black powdery smell that filled an area of his mind that, as a human, he had simply ceased to use, and he wondered if this was how prehistoric man might have experienced scents and smells when out hunting with spear and bow: all of their senses dialed up to maximum as they sought their prey, desperate not to become prey themselves.

Suddenly, something black darted out from a corner of the room that they were passing. Tom quickly leveled the gun and would have squeezed the trigger if Lucien had not calmly raised his hand and lifted the gun up, away from the creature scurrying in the shadows.

"Just a rat," he said, and continued up the corridor.

"I get the impression that this place is full of them," Tom said in a low voice, "and some of them are a hell of a lot bigger and of the two-legged variety." The deep, low growl that came from behind him made the hairs on the back of the Irishman's neck stand to attention.

Lucien walked past the remaining rooms without so much as a glance. He paused at the bottom of the stairs, waiting for Tom and Trey to catch up.

They ascended the stairs, stopping at the top of the first flight at a signal from Lucien, who angled his head, listening for something. Trey turned his own sensory amplifier up to full and let the entire gamut of sounds and smells in

227

the factory wash through him. He heard *everything*. And the sounds, with the scents intricately entwined in and through them, told him that there were creatures on the next floor that were waiting for them: shifting around in the dark shadows, their excitement and their hunger carrying on the musty air as they waited for their opportunity to attack. There was a stench of evil that drifted down from the space above their heads—it oozed slowly down the staircase like a dense black fog, and reminded Trey of the smell of death and decay that he had smelled on Hopper when he had first morphed in his presence.

Lucien sensed it too. He looked at his companions and signaled with a movement of his hand that they were to take the next flight slowly and carefully. He moved off first, silently mounting the tiled steps and motioning for the others to follow. They stopped at the top, tense and alert, anticipating an attack. But none came.

Another darkened corridor stretched out ahead of them, ending with a tall leaded window that allowed the moonlight to peer into the murk—its silver light reflected in hundreds of broken shards of glass on the floor—a broken mosaic of light in the darkness. Halfway up the corridor was a cross-roads. Two perpendicular spurs led off in opposite directions and the meager light coming in from the window was unable to penetrate far into these dark arteries. Somewhere up ahead, something let out a deep throaty rumble, like a tiger's sonorous snarl as it spies the deer through the tall grass. Tom looked around at Trey, flinching slightly at the sight of the giant wolf standing with every muscle tensed, lips curled back to reveal those long, sharp incisors.

Trey opened up the part of his mind that controlled his olfactory senses and tried to locate Alexa's scent again, filtering it out from the myriad of smells in the place. He was certain that she was on this floor, but the scent came from too many directions, as though she had been moved around a lot. The three approached the junction cautiously, until Alexa's piercing scream tore through the silence. They started down the left alley in the direction of the sound and then stopped as a second scream sounded directly behind them.

"Divide and conquer," Tom said.

Lucien nodded. "I'll take this corridor—you and Trey take the other." He paused and gently grabbed Trey by the forearm, looking up into his wolf features. "Stay close to Tom. And remember, I want you to run to safety if anything happens to him. If you manage to get Alexa, remember our plan and get out of here with her as quickly as you can. Good luck, Trey. Don't do anything stupid."

Trey nodded at him, a low growl coming from deep within his chest. Something made him lean forward and lick Lucien's face, his long tongue rasping at the man's beard.

"C'mon, Trey," Tom said, and pulling the werewolf along behind him, they moved off in their opposite directions. Trey paused for a second and glanced behind him as they crossed the junction, watching the back of Lucien as he disappeared into the darkness alone.

24

Lucien continued down the dark corridor, moving cautiously forward until he came to the door that the sound of his
daughter's scream had emanated from. He paused, listening
intently, before pushing it open and stepping quickly into
the room. It was a large open space that had once been used
as some kind of workshop, the remains of workbenches arranged in two rows down the center like giant coffins, the
machinery that had once stood on top of them long since
gone. He scanned the room, peering into the gloom before
moving forward again.

"Daddy, please help me!" Alexa's voice came from behind a door on the far side of the room. The pain woven
through her pleas for help caused Lucien to forget his cau-
tion. He ran toward the sound, throwing open the door and
bursting through to the other side.

He had no sooner placed a foot over the threshold when
the globule hit him in the face.

It expanded instantly to engulf his features, making it
impossible for him to breathe or see. He instinctively raised
his hands to try to tear it off, but his fingers became stuck
in the mass, drawn farther into it and swallowed up as he
struggled to pull them free.

230

He considered misting, but realized that it would be fruitless, as he had no idea how big the room was or where the walls were. To reappear in the middle of a wall, or on the outside of an external one at this height, could be fatal. Besides, there was no point in misting if he couldn't get this damn stuff off his face. And he couldn't get it off.

"Oh, look," Hopper said, his snide voice getting louder as he approached from the other side of the room. "Mr. high-and-mighty Lucien Charron seems to be in a bit of a fix!" His laughter was joined by another's that was deeper and more sinister.

"Having a bit of trouble there, are we?" Hopper continued, now to Lucien's right, but maintaining a cautious distance. "Must be getting quite uncomfortable in there now. Lungs emptying, no oxygen. Even for a vampire, that must be quite a big problem, I'd have thought. What do you reckon, Glebb?"

"Can't see it ranking up there on a vampire's top ten, somehow." Alexa's voice seemed to say these words, but now Lucien knew that his daughter was not in the room, and he knew what the other creature with Hopper was. It was a succubus: a demon capable of perfectly mimicking the voice and appearance of any female in order to lure its male victims to their death. He had been lured into this trap by something as simple as the mimicry of his daughter's cries for help.

"Of course," the succubus continued in Alexa's voice, "him being a nether-creature, even if he dies—if the *undead* can

231

actually be said to die—he'll just rejuve at some point." The voice was mocking, sounding even harsher when vocalized in Alexa's tones, the two demons enjoying the chance to toy with him as he suffocated within the darkness of the mask.

"Oh, Glebb," Hopper said, "have you forgotten? Nether-creatures can be killed by their *own kind*, using nothing more than tooth and claw—or, in this case, spit and cunning."

The two cackled again as they watched Lucien continue to struggle to free himself from the glue-like globe. He began to weaken, and they laughed wildly as his thrashings caused him to fall to the floor. Lying there writhing, his struggles became less and less frantic, until finally they stopped, and he lay motionless in the dust.

The creature called Glebb moved out of the corner it had been hiding in throughout and approached Lucien's prone body. Both demons were in their true form—a temporary bridge had been opened between this world and the Nether-world, incorporating the entire building that they were now in, so they had no need to adopt the cumbersome human *skins* that they normally wore when entering the human plane. The succubus was a tall milky-white creature, devoid of any hair. Its skin didn't appear to fit it properly and hung in great folds at various points on its body. It shuffled as it walked cautiously forward. Looking down at the vampire, it snapped its jaws together twice quickly, the sharp little teeth making an ugly clicking sound as it did so. "Is he dead?" it asked.

232

"Yeah, I reckon. Best make sure though, eh?" the sputum djinn said with an ugly grin.

Hopper stepped forward and raised the wooden stake high above his head. Bringing it down with all his force, he drove it through the vampire's chest.

25

"We should have stuck together," Tom said quietly, walking ahead of Trey into the gloom. "No good can come of us splitting up like this. We're playing right into Caliban's hands."

Trey followed Tom as they carefully approached a door at the end of the short passage. Standing in front of it, Tom readied the gun in his hands, turning on the light mounted just beneath the weapon's muzzle.

Tom nodded up at Trey, his face a mask of concentration. "We don't know what we might be up against here. Caliban knows we are coming, and there's no saying what he might have managed to bring over from the Netherworld with him. Could be anything. Just keep close to me and do exactly as I say, OK?"

The werewolf looked down at him and slowly nodded its head.

Tom looked at the door, took a deep breath, and glanced back at Trey. "How do you want to do this?" he asked with a gesture of his head toward the entrance.

Trey raised his foot and kicked the center of the door. It ripped off both sets of hinges and flew into the center of the empty room on the other side, the tumultuous noise bludgeoning the oppressive silence of the building.

"Oh, the subtle approach," Tom shouted, charging into the room and scanning the corners with the light. Trey ran in after him, ducking under the door frame to stand by his friend's side in the empty room.

"How'd you like that? They invite us to a party and there's nobody here to welcome us."

Something wasn't right. Trey scanned the room again, but there was nothing in any of the dark corners and recesses. There was a pervading stench that filled the room, making him bristle with fear. Tom looked back to him with a wry smile, and then motioned for them to move forward to the double doors in the wall to their left. He hadn't gone more than two steps when the first one fell on him.

"Spiders of Nrgal! Their venom is lethal, Trey. Run!" shouted Tom, twisting his head to the left to avoid the creature's fangs. The giant spider-like creature was the size of a large dog and entirely black, with clusters of onyx-black eyes set into a baleful face. Coarse hairs sprouted from its bulbous body and powerful chitin-covered legs, which it used to grab at Tom from every angle, wrestling him closer toward it in an effort to pierce his flesh with its venomous barbed teeth.

Tom tried to lift the muzzle of the gun to shoot upward into the face of his attacker, but the creature gathered his arm in tightly with one of its legs, making it impossible for him to fire without injuring himself. Having a good purchase on him now, the creature squeezed its prey close and reared its ugly head to deliver the killer bite.

Trey leaped at the beast, his clawed hands closing around the fused head and thorax. He wrenched at the creature's body, but it would not give up its grip on the quarry that it had waited so patiently for. He held on to the head section of the segmented body, struggling to force it back away from Tom and stop those fangs from injecting their deadly poison.

There were others now, scuttling across the ceiling to drop down into the mêlée, their hungry eyes reflecting back the scene below them as they hastened to join the attack.

Trey couldn't pull the thing free of Tom. It took all his effort to simply stop the creature from biting down into his friend—so powerful a grip did it have upon him. He roared his anger and frustration and bit down into the creature's head, hoping that the pain might distract it enough to let go of Tom. There was a sickening pop as one of the giant spider-creature's eyes burst, followed by a keening screech. The creature writhed in agony, all of its legs moving at once, and it let go of Tom and turned on Trey with incredible speed.

As it turned, lifting its longer front legs to grab at him, Trey briefly glimpsed the soft underside of its abdomen. He hooked his fingers and raked them down into the leathery flesh, sinking his claws deep into the tissue beneath and opening up a cavernous wound. The contents of the creature's body sagged to the floor and hung beneath it like some gruesome pendulum. Trey wrenched his hand free

236

and watched as the creature fell to the floor, a black tar-like substance quickly surrounding its dead corpse.

"Too many of them, Trey. Quick, run," Tom shouted, indicating the approaching figures overhead. He pushed Trey toward the double doors, spraying the ceiling with bullets—the percussion of the machine gun in the enclosed room a roaring cacophony of noise that caused Trey to wince in pain as the sound assaulted his ears.

They ran to the doors, stopping long enough for Tom to tear loose one of the grenades from his jerkin. He ripped the pin free and rolled it toward the creatures that were now advancing at them across the floor. As soon as the grenade left his hand he grabbed Trey by the arm and pushed him through the doors, closing them and taking refuge behind the wall that they were set into. The power of the explosion within the confines of the room was enormous—a wall of noise and smoke smashed through the doors as the explosive shock wave ripped through everything in its destructive path. Tom, who had been crouched over the hulking figure of Trey, was up in a fraction of a second, firing round after round into the smoke until the magazine was empty.

He ducked back down against Trey and changed the clip. The two of them eventually got to their feet and cautiously peered into the clearing smoke to see pieces of the spider demons scattered everywhere.

The sound of hands clapping behind them made them whirl around to face the source of the noise. A tall, luminously pale creature stood facing them, regarding them through glowing eyes that promised nothing but death. The twin pools of hatred never stopped gazing at Trey for a second, and the teenager knew without a doubt that he was looking at the creature that wanted him destroyed: Caliban.

"My, we do like to make an entrance, don't we?"

26

Hopper looked down at Lucien's dead body and shook his head in disgust.

"Vampires. Jumped-up ponces, the lot of them," he said. "Supposed to be the 'dark lords of the night'—pah! Taken out by nothing more than a woman's voice and a bit of demon cunning."

"I'd be careful what you say about his kind with Caliban in the same building, Hopper. He has a way of hearing these things, you know," Glebb said in his own voice now, sidling over to him.

"I'd have preferred it if that human scum, Tom, had been the one to come this way," Hopper said. "I'd have enjoyed ripping him apart piece by bloody piece. I can taste him now. But I'll have him, you mark my words. As a reward for dealing with *this*," he said, nodding toward the dead figure on the floor in front of him, "Caliban will let me have him, you see if he don't. I'll drink his blood, I will." He clicked his teeth together and smiled at the thought.

"Talking of blood, there's not much coming out of him really, is there?" Glebb said, pointing at the prone figure of the vampire.

Hopper looked down again, screwing up his hobgoblin

features. "No, not really. I reckon the stake must be keeping it from coming out too much."

"What do we do with him now?" Glebb said, tentatively prodding at the body with a clawed foot while maintaining his distance.

"Caliban said that we've got to burn him. But he wants to see the body first, so we'll have to drag him through from here. Come on, grab a leg." Hopper started to reach down to pull the body by the feet, but stopped, realizing that it wasn't going to go anywhere while it was pinioned to the floor by the wooden stake sticking out of the torso.

"Take that thing out, will you?" Hopper said to the succubus.

"I'm not touching it. You staked him. You clear up your own mess."

Hopper glared at the other demon. "You know why you succubi are despised and derided by other demons, don't you? Because you don't have any balls—like the women you imitate!" He cackled at his own joke and crabbed his way around the body to remove the stake.

Hopper stepped forward and placed his foot on the vampire's chest. He wrapped his hands around the heavy wooden pole and pulled up as hard as he could.

It was the last thing he ever did.

As soon as Hopper's foot came into contact with Lucien, the gluey mass on the vampire's face changed form. Lucien, who had been battling so hard not to slip over the edge of consciousness into death's dark abyss, seized upon the only chance that he knew he might get. He tore the suffocating glob from his face and drew a huge ragged breath, his mouth and eyes open impossibly wide as he sucked in the air. He shook the remainder of the substance from his hand and in the same movement grabbed Hopper's leg by the ankle, locking his muscles to ensure that there would be no escape from his grip. The foul nether-creature's pupils constricted to black pinpricks as he looked down and witnessed the reanimation of his nemesis.

With his free hand, Lucien wrenched the stake from his chest, the pain a deafening wall of white noise that consumed everything else and forced a roar of agony from him. He looked up at the sharp wooden tool and wondered at how he had survived being skewered by such a horrendous instrument.

When the stake had been driven into his chest, narrowly missing his heart, he had had to close down huge areas of his consciousness to escape the raging avalanche of pain that had threatened to crush him. He had retreated from it, finding a small refuge in his mind from which he could look out on the bedlam that ensued, and he hid there, waiting and trying to stay alive long enough to escape should an opportunity arise. But now, forced out of his refuge, the tortuous pain was back again, eating through him like a forest fire gobbling up everything in its path.

Struggling to his feet, he held Hopper aloft in one hand, dangling the demon upside down above the floor. The sputum djinn had regained its wits now, and spat globule after globule at Lucien, twisting this way and that to get the shots in. But it was pointless. As long as Lucien was in contact with him, the balls of gunk simply failed to stick, sliding off harmlessly instead.

A stream of blood ran down Lucien's back and front, sticking his trousers to his legs. He felt his knees buckle, threatening to give way beneath him, but he straightened up again and shook the demon by the leg.

"Goodbye, Hopper," he said, and throwing the demon to the floor, he reunited Hopper with the wooden stake, slamming the sharpened pole through his body. He looked on impassively as the demon squirmed for a second and then sank back, dead.

He turned slowly, seeking out the succubus. The creature had slunk away into the darkened corner that it had first come from. It looked back at Lucien, imploring eyes scanning the face of the vengeful monster standing in front of it.

"Tell me," Lucien said in a level voice.

"No, I can't. Please, you can't make me," the demon said, shrinking away from him.

"Your name, Succubus!"

"Please, no—"

"Tell me your true demon name, Succubus," Lucien repeated, pulling the bloody stake from the dead body of the sputum djinn. "Tell me your name, or his death will be yours too."

242

The creature looked into his eyes for pity, but there was none to be found in those burning globes of hate. Lucien took a step toward him, raising the stake over his head.

"My name is Rashishnrok," the succubus said quickly, holding his hands out in front of his face as if to fend off the inevitable attack.

Lucien nodded slowly and lowered the stake. "You know the covenant of the Netherworld. Now that I know your true demon name, you are mine. *I* am your master now, and you will obey my every word. You are to return to the Netherworld and never come again to the human plane unless I summon you. If you do, I will enter your name into the Book of Halzog and he will come to claim you."

He turned his back on the pathetic creature.

"Go. And remember who your true master is now."

The creature slowly disappeared until only the merest shadow of it could be detected in the darkness, before that too faded away.

Lucien sank to his knees. A gasp escaped him, and his body refused to respond to his commands. He had lost too much blood. The stake had narrowly missed his heart but had gone through a lung, and the damage was massive. His wounds were hemorrhaging profusely.

He lay down. He was too tired and he wanted nothing more than to allow the coldness that had started to creep through his body to engulf him utterly.

His eyes jerked open at the explosion, and he listened as

the sound of Tom's gun tore through the blackness that had started to descend upon him.

With an effort, he got back up onto his hands and knees and started to crawl toward the noise.

27

As Lucien crawled back through the filth of the corridor, the sooty dust that covered the floors mixed with the blood on his hands and clothes, coating them with an inky, sticky mess.

He was mindful of the constant flow of blood from his chest and back. He knew that he was able to lose a great deal of blood before his body would simply shut down and cease to function, but he tried not to think about how close he must be to that point. This shutting down was the reason that he was alive now, but it would be no good for him to enter this state while he was certain that Tom and Trey were in mortal danger and that Alexa was still in his brother's hands.

When Hopper had attacked him, he realized that there was no point in struggling against the suffocation. He thought that if he could convince them that he was already dead, he might be able to avoid the inevitable staking. He had sunk to the floor and closed off almost all his body functions, reducing his heartbeat to nearly a complete stop. He did this while remaining alert to the movements of the two creatures in the room with him. It was a similar state to that which he was able to place himself in when he "slept"—

effectively putting his vampire body into a sort of stasis. In this way, he had been able to reduce the loss of blood to a minimum and almost ignore his inability to breathe.

When the stake had been driven through him, the pain had been incredible, but he was able to bear it due to the almost complete lack of bodily function, and he would have been capable of staying like that for some considerable time. But when Hopper had inadvertently released him from the suffocating mask, he knew that he would have to take his chances and try to get free.

He had come out of the stasis very fast, ramping up the body functions necessary to react quickly and seizing his chance to dispatch the demon. And that had left him with so very little strength and life force that simply crawling was difficult now, and the blood loss was becoming more serious by the second.

He arrived at the junction of the central corridor and stopped, propping himself up against a wall. He reached down and tore a long strip of material out of his trousers, ripping them from the hem to the top of his thigh. He roughly balled the material up and jammed as much as he could into the gaping wound in his chest, hoping to stem some of the flow.

He started off again, this time going down the fork that Trey and Tom had taken, crawling through the doorway into the room at the end.

He noticed the door lying broken inside the room and moved ahead as quickly as he could. He stopped, seeing the figure of the giant spider, and slowly moved toward it, noting the pool of viscous substance that had bled from its body. Other pieces of spider bodies lay scattered around in among spent cartridge shells, and Lucien guessed that the carnage was the result of the explosion that he had heard. Relief washed through him when he realized that none of the bodies was that of Tom or Trey.

He crawled forward again through the filth and debris that littered the floor, forcing his limbs to respond to his will. But there was nothing left in him to call upon any longer—his strength gave out and he collapsed, his arms buckling under him and his face crunching painfully into the floor. Gulping the stagnant air into his one working lung, he finally succumbed to the black mist that swirled in and around him and waited for his long existence to come to an end.

His brother's voice cut through the darkness, the sound of it reaching out and stopping Lucien from completely sliding down under the murky surface that he had begun to slip beneath. The voice had a harsh, guttural quality, like a saw cutting through bone, and it was utterly without humor, or passion, or pity. It was a voice that had existed on this earth for almost three hundred years, and had during that time threatened nothing but death—or worse—to all who had been unfortunate enough to hear it. It was the voice that had accompanied Lucien throughout his early existence, when it had encouraged, cajoled, and spurred him on to greater excesses of blood and misery. It was a voice that he had foolishly listened to and believed in for so long, until one day he had witnessed its owner commit an atrocity so horrific and foul that something inside Lucien had snapped. He had vowed that he would never listen to it again, but instead endeavor to silence it forever and remove its poison from the world. With sadness he realized that he had ultimately failed in this, and that it would be his own voice that ceased to be heard.

The roar that cut through the oppressive quiet that followed could only be Trey, and the sound stirred something in Lucien that was a perfect counterpoint to the hopelessness that he had begun to embrace. He formed a picture of Alexa in his mind and used this to push a way through the pain and despair that had threatened to consume him so utterly. On top of this, he considered the terrifying possibility of Tom and Trey trying to rescue her from his brother without his help and he knew that he could not allow this to happen.

Lucien closed his eyes and sucked in a deep, ragged breath. He drew upon some deeply hidden reserve of strength and somehow managed to pull himself up off the floor. On his knees, he ignored the waves of dizziness that engulfed him as he determinedly struggled to get his foot underneath him. Slowly he stood up, wavering on the spot like a drunk.

A small gasp escaped his lips as he forced his foot forward, this insignificant action causing new waves of pain to course through his body. He forced himself to lift his head and straighten up to his full height, ignoring the new streams of blood that sprang forth and flowed down his front and back as a result. Walking toward the open door up ahead, he proceeded in the direction of his brother's voice.

28

Tom and Trey turned around to look at Caliban. He was standing in the center of the room. A small skylight in the ceiling allowed the moonlight to pick him out, like a spotlight trained upon the lead actor in a play. Alexa was standing by his side. She appeared to be unhurt, but her eyes were dull and vacant as though she was under the influence of some powerful narcotic.

Trey could see *things* moving in the shadows of the room, shades and shadows suggesting the forms of creatures that were not quite solid enough to make out. They were communicating with each other. A babbling, discordant din of jumbled voices and animal noises that all sounded at the same time, making it impossible to pick out anything of meaning.

"Silence!" Caliban commanded, and the voices dropped to a barely audible whisper.

Trey turned to see Tom raise his gun and aim at the vampire. Trey reached out to stop him as Caliban swiftly pulled Alexa in front of him. The Irishman held his fire, keeping his finger resting on the trigger, hoping for a chance to let off a round into the vampire.

Caliban was as tall as his brother. And, like Lucien, his

head was also completely bald. But that was where any similarity between the brothers ended.

Caliban looked ancient. His skin was gray and stretched tight over his skull, revealing sharp cheekbones and a jutting jaw. His eyes, set in sunken pockets, were yellow adulterations of the fascinating pools of color that were Lucien's, and the pupils were black and elongated like those of a goat.

He smiled at them from over the girl's shoulder, his upper lip peeling back over the ivory-white fangs that protruded from his mouth. He raised his hand and began to stroke at Alexa's throat with long, blackened talons, the slow, deliberate movement putting a stop to any thoughts that Tom or Trey might have had of launching any kind of attack. He watched their reactions as he pressed the hooked claws into the flesh and raked his fingers along the smooth surface, leaving white scratches but not breaking the skin.

He tut-tutted and slowly shook his head in Tom's direction. "Why so aggressive?" Caliban asked in a wounded tone. His voice was calm, but the menace behind it wound in among the words. "Surely we can talk about all this in a *civilized* way?"

He looked at the gun in Tom's hands and pouted in disappointment, like a teacher who has caught his pupil coming to school with a penknife. "Besides, what do you hope to accomplish with your little peashooters, hmmm? Apart from making a rather unsightly mess, they really are of no use to you here, you foolish little *human*." He looked deep

251

into Tom's eyes, and the ugly smile returned. "But you already know that, don't you, hmm? The gun is merely a means to an end, isn't it? A tool to buy you some time so that you can try to stick me like some pig with one of those terrible wooden stakes that you have no doubt brought." He rolled his eyes theatrically. "How utterly predictable. You pathetic, insignificant little man."

He motioned with the fingers of his free hand, and a mass of thick black tendrils shot out from the shadows of the wall and instantly engulfed the Irishman, pulling him up off his feet and dragging him back into their inky darkness.

"Uh-uh," he said to Trey, with a small shake of his head, as the werewolf made to go to his friend's aid.

Trey watched helplessly as the snake-like shapes wrapped themselves around Tom's arms and legs, one coiling itself around his neck and mouth, pulling his head toward it in a constrictor's embrace. Tom's eyes bulged slightly at the pressure on his throat, but they flicked quickly from Caliban to Trey, warning the boy to be careful.

Caliban shook his head in a show of irritation. He turned his attention to Trey, continuing to stroke at Alexa's throat as he spoke.

"All this violence. It really is so unnecessary, don't you agree, Mr. Laporte?" He looked up at the werewolf and raised his eyebrows slightly. "I believe that we should be able to talk about things and come to some sort of . . . amnesty. Is that unreasonable of me, Trey? You don't mind if I call you Trey, do you?"

252

Tom made a muffled sound to his left, but Trey couldn't take his eyes off the claws on Alexa's throat.

"Silence, you dog!" Caliban shouted in Tom's direction, without taking his eyes from Trey's. "Or I shall have you permanently removed from the proceedings.

"The problem with these *humans*," he continued, "is that they do not understand their real position in this world. They believe that they are the ultimate beings, that evolution has produced in them the pinnacle of existence. What they do not realize is that to be the ultimate being in your environment, you must first occupy the very top of the food chain and that you must rule over all the other creatures that you as the ultimate predator deem fit to share your world. Sadly they have lost sight of the fact that they are not at the pinnacle of this hierarchy: I and my kind are above them in the pecking order. To me, they are nothing but prey, a livestock that my kind have feasted upon for thousands of years. I despise them all."

He glanced momentarily at Tom before fixing Trey with his devil eyes again.

"My brother has no doubt tried to convince you that I am evil incarnate—that I would happily eradicate humankind and turn this world into a very different kind of place. Indeed, I have the power to do this. I have the Ring of Amon and, if I chose to, I could have them tear this world of theirs apart. So why have I not done so?"

Trey noticed for the first time the large silver ring on the middle finger of the hand around Alexa's neck.

"Come now, Trey, this conversation really is a little one-sided. Change back to your human form so that we can talk and sort this mess out."

Tom made a noise again, and Caliban, not taking his eyes from Trey, strangled the sound with the tiniest movement of his finger.

"I am too old to fight anymore. I am almost three hundred years of age and I no longer wish for conflict. I want an end to this warring between my brother and me, and I believe that you alone might be able to broker this peace. So, please, change back to your human form so that we can talk, and I will let Alexa and your friend go."

He looked up at Trey imploringly. "If I had wanted to hurt your friends, don't you think that I could have done so already? I just want to talk. Talk to me, Trey. Help me find a way to put an end to all of this."

Trey fingered the silver amulet around his neck. He looked at Alexa and the emptiness in her eyes and pictured how Caliban had raked his talons across her flesh only moments before. He cast a glance toward Tom, his heart sinking as he saw his friend's lifeless body consumed by the blackness of the shadow creatures.

Trey was on his own. There was no way he could see of breaking this stalemate without complying with Caliban's demands.

He morphed back to his human form.

The second he did so, the walls seemed to come alive, and the black, foul creatures started to emerge—sliding and crawling into the room. They slithered and slunk out of the darkness, the babbling, discordant noise increasing as they did so. Trey believed that the hordes of hell were descending upon him, so grotesque were the beasts that began to approach.

"No, Trey! It's a trap, he wants to kill us all. Change back!" Alexa's eyes, which had been fixed on the floor since they had entered, suddenly came alive and looked up at him as her voice filled his head.

"Shut up, you little *witch*!" Caliban's voice cut like a knife across Alexa's, and Trey watched as the vampire savagely pulled back Alexa's head, rearing his own away, lips pulled back over those monstrous teeth, ready to rend the tender flesh of the girl's neck.

Time seemed to stretch outward as what happened next unraveled. Trey felt as though he was rooted to the spot as he watched Caliban launch his attack. His muscles would not respond to his demands to go to Alexa's aid, and he watched in horror as Caliban, his mouth open impossibly wide, lowered his head toward Alexa's exposed throat.

And suddenly Lucien was between them.

He misted between his brother and his daughter, his blood-caked body shielding the girl from the monster's bite. Caliban's teeth sank deep into his sibling. But instead of trying to push him away, Lucien reached up, wrapping his arms around his brother's head and pulling it tight into him, sinking the fangs deeper into his own flesh and making it impossible for the other to break loose.

Alexa sank to the floor, and Trey watched as Caliban struggled against his brother's harsh embrace, raking his clawed fingers against Lucien's head and opening up great, ugly wounds that immediately transformed into flowing valleys of blood. The older vampire, unable to wrench himself free, misted to escape the fraternal clinch. Trey watched as Lucien did likewise. But something was terribly wrong. Caliban blinked out and reappeared almost instantly no more than two feet in front of Trey, looking as if he had succeeded in his attempt to be free. But his head was still buckled forward at the awkward angle that Lucien had held it in, and Caliban looked to Trey like a man who had somehow broken his neck, only to discover that he would be forced to hold it in this grotesque, lopsided position forever. Caliban's eyes were peering upward, as though looking for the invisible force that seemed to hold him still. Then the air in front of him seemed to swell and burn, shimmering as it coalesced into the thing that was Lucien Charron as he re-formed in the exact same position that he had held before he'd disappeared.

Trey remembered what Tom had told him about the flicker that he had witnessed when he had fought Lucien during their training session, and how this had signaled Lucien's growing weariness. Trey knew that if that flicker had signaled the vampire was tiring, this slow emergence into re-existence must signal that Lucien would not be capable of holding his brother much longer and would certainly be incapable of misting again.

Lucien's breath was coming in deep ragged gasps, and as Trey watched he opened his eyes against the pain and looked over in his direction. The look that he gave Trey made the boy's heart sink. It was a look of complete and utter exhaustion and defeat. Trey's guardian was unable to hold on any longer and would at any moment succumb to death at his brother's hands.

As if sensing this, Caliban formed his right hand into a spear, his fingers forced together so that those sharp claws formed a row of forward-facing daggers, and prepared to plunge them into his brother's exposed neck.

The hand reared back in anticipation of the strike, coming within an inch of accidentally striking Trey in the face. He jerked his head back to avoid the blow, and this instinctive act was enough to shake him free from the paralyzing fear that had petrified him from the moment he thought Caliban was about to murder Alexa. He instantly morphed and lunged forward, clamping his wolf jaws around Caliban's arm and sinking his teeth into the flesh. A muffled scream went up from the vampire, but Trey ignored it, biting down harder through skin and muscle and blood vessels, transferring all the immense power in his jaws through his white, chisel teeth. Caliban flailed out with his legs, kicking out and issuing a screech of unadulterated agony, while Lucien somehow maintained the vise-like grip on his head, making it impossible for him to get away or defend himself. Trey fought the need to gag as the vampire's foul blood spewed from the wound into his mouth. He instinctively knew that he must not swallow—he closed off the back of his throat to stop any of the poisonous filth from being ingested, allowing it to pour freely through the closing gap between his jaws. Finally, with a loud crack and a splintering of bone, Trey's teeth met again and the vampire's hand dropped at his feet with a thud, just as Lucien's strength and will finally gave out and he let go of his brother, collapsing to the floor as if dead.

The scream was like the howl of a jet engine at takeoff, so utterly did it fill the room. It came not just from Caliban, but also from the shadow creatures that had crept from the walls, and it crushed the air that vibrated with its noise. Trey clamped his hands to his ears, watching as the demon creatures slunk back toward the shadows. A strange, uncomfortable *wrenching* sensation seemed to pull at every molecule that was in and of the room and the people within it, as though the elastic of the universe had suddenly been stretched too far and the cosmos was protesting against the force. There was a *snap* that sucked the air out of Trey's lungs like he'd been hit in the solar plexus, and when he looked up, the shadow creatures and their evil leader had disappeared.

Alexa crawled over to her father's body, lifting his head so that she could cradle it in her lap—tears tracked down her face and fell from her chin onto Lucien's blood-soaked clothing.

"Is he dead?" Trey asked, kneeling down beside her. Human again now, he shivered, and not merely against the cold.

258

"No. But he will be if we don't get him help immediately." She looked up at him and nodded. "Thank you, Trey, you saved him." She placed her hand on his and smiled at him through her tears.

A cough from behind him signaled that Tom was somehow still alive, and Trey jumped up and ran to his friend. He helped him back to his feet and watched as he gingerly reached up to feel the angry red and purple lesions around his neck.

"Tom, I thought you were done for."

"Me? No. It takes more than having the bejaysus strangled out of me by some hell-creature-from-the-pit to do away with Yours Truly. We Irish are made out of tough stuff, you know." He coughed, wincing painfully, before he looked up and noticed Lucien on the floor.

The Irishman grabbed for the walkie-talkie in his pocket. After speaking to Jens, he put the device back in his pocket and stood with Trey, looking down at the bloody body in Alexa's arms.

"They're coming, Lucien," Trey said in a small voice. "Hold on."

Tom turned to Trey. The anxiety in his eyes was clear to see, but he nodded his head in the boy's direction and smiled grimly. "You did well, Trey. Better than well."

Trey shook his head and looked down at Lucien. "I should have acted sooner. I just stood there frozen. I could have stopped that," he said with a gesture of his head toward his guardian.

"You acted when you had to. If you hadn't, we'd all be dead now."

"But he got away."

"That's true enough," Tom said, walking across the room. He bent down and picked something up, holding it out for Trey to examine. "But he left this behind."

Tom held up the severed remains of Caliban's hand. Ragged strips of flesh hung from what had once been the wrist, and the fingers were clawed, as if, even now, it was intent on committing some act of violence.

"And would you look at that," Tom said. He pulled the ring off of the middle finger, throwing the severed limb back to the floor in disgust. "The Ring of Amon. Trey, you're an honest-to-God bloody marvel, so you are."

He very carefully placed the ring in one of the zipped pockets of his jacket and fastened it.

Outside, the snare-drum sound of a helicopter's rotor blades signaled Jens's arrival.

Trey stood looking down at the broken figure that was Lucien. Tears welled up in his eyes and he blinked them away. Tom moved over to him and placed an arm around his shoulder, pulling him into him in a friendly embrace. "C'mon," he said. "Let's get him home."

The huge helicopter landed in the scrubland at the back of the factory. Trey watched as the metal leviathan descended out of the heavens, its downdraft kicking up the dust from the dry ground and creating a thick, gray cloud that

260

stung his eyes and throat. He pulled the jacket that Jens had brought from the car around himself, and watched as the rescue operation unfolded.

Jens and his men quickly managed to get Lucien onto a stretcher and into the helicopter, where a medic did his best to staunch the flow of blood and make Lucien as comfortable as possible through the administration of drugs. They ushered Tom, Alexa, and Trey into the body of the aircraft, next to him, and within minutes the giant craft was airborne again. Alexa never let go of her father's hand throughout the short journey to the airport. She only looked up once, smiling bravely at Tom and Trey as they were landing, but the deep worry etched on her face told them that she didn't believe that her father was going to make it.

Jens had called ahead, so that when they arrived at the airport a doctor was waiting on the tarmac, and Lucien was given the blood that he so desperately needed. The doctor and Jens exchanged worried glances, and Alexa was warned about not taking him back to London too soon. But Lucien had opened his eyes then and squeezed his daughter's hand. Alexa bent toward him, and he had simply said, "Home," before falling back into unconsciousness.

So the arrangements were hastily made and the jet took all four of them back to London, where they were met by a private ambulance and taken to the apartment in Docklands.

EPILOGUE

It was three weeks before Lucien opened his eyes again. When he did, it was Trey who was in the room with him, sitting in a chair reading, the gap between them filled with the various drips and machines that were wired into the motionless body laid out upon the bed.

He and Alexa were taking it in turns to sit by his bedside, and Alexa was out with Tom looking for a new type of mattress for Lucien.

Trey detected the tiniest movement out of the corner of his eye, and when he looked up, Lucien was awake.

He looked very small and his skin seemed papery thin against the cotton pillowcases. There was very little to reconcile the figure on the bed with the imposing individual that Trey had first met at the care home. It was as if the essence of Lucien had been sucked out of his body and all that was left was this frail husk.

Trey jumped up and moved over to the bed, taking hold of Lucien's hand. His guardian's eyes flicked toward him, and a trace of a smile played upon his lips.

"Trey—" Lucien whispered.

"Shh, Lucien. I'll go and get the nurse." Trey went to move away but the grip on his hand strengthened, pulling him back.

"No. Tell me, is Alexa OK?"

"Yes, Lucien. You saved her. She was unharmed." Trey smiled down at him and watched as the eyes fluttered and closed again. He looked toward the paging device on the bed and thought about pressing the button to summon the medical staff, who were on twenty-four-hour call and who had set up base in one of the offices below.

When he looked back, Lucien's eyes were fixed on him again.

"The Ring of Amon?" he whispered.

"Tom had it destroyed the very next day. He and two of his people took it to a smelting plant. He said that dropping that thing into the furnace was one of the most satisfying things he'd ever done." Trey smiled at the memory of the Irishman retelling the story and how his eyes had lit up as he described watching the ring disappear into the molten metal.

"Good. That's good," Lucien said, nodding his head slightly.

"Shall I call Alexa? She and Tom could jump in a cab and be here in no time. She'll be mortified that she wasn't here when you came to."

Lucien shook his head and looked up at him sadly.

"Do you need anything, Lucien?" Trey asked anxiously. "Is there anything that I can do for you?"

"I'm dying, Trey. There is nothing that you or anyone else can do about that." He pulled Trey closer. "You are a very special person, Trey Laporte, and I am sad that we will not have much more time together. Tell Alexa that I love her."

He closed his eyes and drifted back into unconsciousness, his hand slipping away from Trey's. Trey looked at him and grabbed for the medical pager.

Alexa blamed herself for not being there when her father had come around and vowed that she would not leave the room again—she would sleep in the chair at night to be with him.

In the days that followed, the three of them—Alexa, Trey, and Tom—drifted around the apartment, desperately trying not to hover outside Lucien's room, but rushing up to question any medical staff that came to the door for news about his condition.

At dinner one evening, they all sat around the table in the kitchen doing their best to seem interested in the food that Mrs. Magilton had put out for them. They had not discussed what Lucien had said about his dying, but this evening Alexa brought it up and asked Trey to repeat what her father had said. Tom was unusually quiet, tapping at his bottom lip with the handle of his spoon, lost in thought, and not joining in with their discussion about Lucien's health.

Eventually, Trey couldn't take it anymore. "Tom, what is it that you know and aren't telling us?"

"Hmmm? Oh, I was just thinking about what Lucien said about nobody being able to help him."

"And . . ."

"Well, it's not quite true. There is somebody who is able to help him."

Trey's heart gave a little flutter at the way that Tom had said this, and he looked intensely at the older man.

"Who is it, Tom? Who can help him?"

Tom looked at the table, before glancing back at the two teenagers staring intently at him.

"Alexa's mother. Lucien's wife, Gwendolin." The words came out of his mouth like an apology, and the big Irishman looked down at his plate.

Alexa shook her head. "My mother's dead," she said.

"She isn't dead, Alexa," Tom said. "Your father told you that to make it easier for you to forget her. She left your father for Caliban. She's his sorceress."

"You're lying."

"I'm sorry that I had to tell you this, Alexa. Your father didn't wish for you to know what she had become. She has changed so much. But she has an item—Mynor's Globe—which is the only thing that might be able to save Lucien's life."

"Then we have to get it," Trey said. "How do we find her?"

Tom still had his eyes glued to Alexa. "She lives in a place that straddles this world and the Netherworld. It's called the Tower of Leroth, but it will be no easy task to even get there, let alone steal the globe from her. The estate has no static location, but changes its position as it forms new bridges between the demon plane and this one."

Silence hung over the room like a curse.

"How could this item help Lucien?" Trey asked, breaking the spell.

"It has extraordinary powers of healing. Especially for nether-creatures. I believe that it could restore Lucien to full health again."

Alexa stood up, the scrape of her chair against the ceramic tiles cutting through the kitchen like a saw. The two men looked up at her, waiting to see what would happen next.

"Then what are we waiting for?" she said. "We'd better work out how we are going to reunite me with my 'dead' mother and save my father's life."

Tom also stood up, his face set resolutely. "We also have a traitor to find. And believe me, when I do, they'll wish that they had never heard the name of Lucien Charron."

DEMONCYCLOPEDIA

A GUIDE TO THE NETHERWORLD
AND ITS CREATURES

INTRODUCTION

Relations between the human realm and the Netherworld have always been complex and secretive, distorted by myth and the dark art of storytelling. Rarely have they been openly aggressive. Demons have always lived among us (you may think you have met one or two). For most of our history, the comings and goings of the Netherworld's hellish inhabitants were strictly controlled by the all-powerful demon lords who ruled over them—not because the demon lords held any love for the human race, but because it served their interests to control the portal between the worlds. The realms coexisted, with secret contracts and treaties governing their contact and occasional violent skirmishes when these were breached. But the events documented in this book show that we are in a new era: The vampire Caliban and his cohort are bolder and more aggressive, the demon lords hold no sway over them, and the old lore is no longer relevant.

It may be useful for you to know more about the foe we are facing, so with the help of Lucien Charron's researchers, we have compiled a basic guide to the creatures of the Netherworld for humans new to demon life and lore.

VAMPIRES

(Netherworld slang names: *vamps*, *bloodjunkies*, *leeches*, *hemoholics*)

Descendants of an ancient race, vampires have lived among humankind since time began. They see themselves as the ultimate predators—and humans as little more than another link in their food chain. They need us for survival, and, in a sense, this gives us an advantage over them. Through the centuries, humans have hunted them down and destroyed them or banished them to the Netherworld. But their bloodlust will always drive them back to the human realm.

Now the vampires have risen to power within the Netherworld, vanquishing the old demon lords. They want to use their power to raise an army of nether-creatures and ultimately to rule in the human realm.

Physical characteristics: Pale and wan (especially when hungry) with extraordinary eyes that possess an almost hypnotic quality. Heliophobes, they are unable to withstand exposure to direct sunlight—short exposures causing scalding and blistering of the skin, longer exposures resulting in total combustion. Can live to incalculable ages, and usually their years do not show—unless their lives have been particularly cruel and bloody. Male vampires can be remarkably attractive to human women. Permanent fangs and talons make them easy to spot in a crowd.

Methods of dispatching a vamp: Staking—the traditional option and still the best. However, driving a sharp instrument through the chest is not enough; the heart must be pierced. Beheading—usually carried out as part of a staking. While not strictly necessary (each method is perfectly effective on its own), it's better to be safe rather than sorry when dealing with the undead. Fire/Explosives—total annihilation of the body using flame or explosives. Drowning—in water or oil.

Myths: Mirrors—all vampires have reflections. Sleeping in coffins (who in their right mind would choose to sleep in a coffin?). Ability to shape-shift into bats/wolves/snakes.

WEREWOLVES

(Netherworld slang names: *lycos*, *wolfmen*, *furboys*, *helldogs*)

Wolf/human shape-shifters enslaved to the power of the full moon. The usual lycanthrope form is the Wolfan, which is ferocious and formidable but has no control over its urges to kill and feed during the full moon. Much rarer is the lyco who can adopt the bimorphic form, which means they can transform at will. The bimorph stands upright, in full control of its powers, combining the force of the human mind with the physical power of the beast. This hybrid form, however, can only be achieved by naturals (hereditary werewolves born to two werewolf parents) who wear an Amulet of Theiss.* Huge and powerful creatures with super-acute senses, they are among the very few creatures (nether or human) feared by vampires.

Physical characteristics: In human form indistinguishable from other humans. In wolf form the most powerful beast imaginable: larger than an average wolf, with thick glistening fur, killer jaws; thoroughly animal. The bimorph will have wolf/human hybrid limbs, with an extraordinarily powerful animal upper body and head. Its sense of hearing, smell, and sight will be exceptional.

Methods of dispatching a lyco: Remarkably similar to vamps—fire, beheading, drowning.

Myths: Silver bullets are not effective. And not necessarily fans of rare meat.

*Amulets containing wolfsbane. Originating in the sixteenth century, these lend the wearer great control and enhance their bimorphic powers.

DEMONS AND DJINN

The most numerous and varied of the nether-creatures, demons and djinn make up over ninety percent of the Netherworld's population. Some have inhabited the Netherworld as long as it has existed; others have been created—summoned into existence by sorcerers and practitioners of dark magic. A vast hierarchy exists for demons and djinn, the cause of many fights and even wars in the history of the realm. Demons are by far the most powerful group, with djinn often submissive and obsequious in their company. While not as powerful, djinn are far more numerous, and this imbalance between power and population has been a major source of friction between the two groups.

The most powerful demons, with their knowledge of magic, are extremely difficult to kill, but every demon has an Achilles' heel: a unique and secret name that was given to it at its creation. They guard and cherish this name above all else, knowing that should it ever be discovered, they are forever bound to obey the commands of the individual (demon or human) who has used it.

While technically separate orders of nether-creatures, the djinn like to consider themselves as "true demons" (even referring to themselves as such and inventing their own caste-like system of nomenclature). Demons, on the other hand, consider the djinn as being lesser in worth, power, and status. The demon hierarchy is a complicated system, separating demon species into strict categories that determine role and status in the Netherworld.

DEMON HIERARCHY

Level-Four Demons: The most powerful demons. An elite echelon that has traditionally ruled over the Netherworld. Hell-Krakens, Pit Shedim, Infernals, and Terrorfiends are among this group.

Level-Three Demons: Still important, these demons are often found in positions of prominence in the Netherworld. Examples include Shadow demons, Bone Grells, Ghuls, Ashnon, and Murkbeasts.

Level-Two Demons: The majority of demons fall into this group. Incubi, Nargwan, Succubi, Maug, Hordelings, Necrotrophs, etc.

Level-One Demons: The lowest echelon of demon society, these creatures often lead wretched lives, existing only to carry out the work that others would not consider doing. Orgons, Krell, and Sprites are all examples.

The djinn also have a four-level system of nomenclature, although this is dismissed by the demon communities. To them (even to the lowly level-one demons), the djinn are little more than upstarts and underlings—creatures created with relatively simple magic that have spread and multiplied to problematic numbers in the Netherworld.

The diversity in both demon and djinn orders is further complicated by how these creatures must adapt to cross over into the human realm: Both species are separated into *indies* and *deeps*. Independents are capable of existing in the human realm on their own, adopting a human mantle to disguise themselves. Deeps, or dependents, must take possession of a human body to live in the human realm; like parasites, these creatures move from host to host, indifferent to whatever death or madness they leave in their wake.

EXAMPLES OF INDIES

Maug: Large, powerful demons. Not particularly intelligent, but ferocious fighting skills and a powerful sense of loyalty to any employer make them the ideal choice for security and bodyguard work.

Shadow Demons: Impossibly fast, these demons revel in their reputation as ruthless killers. They often set themselves up as mercenaries or assassins for hire. They are particularly effective in darkened places, where their skin seems to absorb any light, making them impossible to see until it is too late. They are effective killing machines.

Incubi/Succubi: Shape-shifting demons able to take on the appearance and attributes of men and women respectively. They have a unique ability to perceive their intended victim's fantasies and desires and adopt a disguise to lure them. At heart they are cowardly, but they feed on the gullible and conceited and are widely used to infiltrate the worlds of the wealthy and glamorous.

EXAMPLES OF DEEPS

Necrotrophs: Parasitic creatures. They infest their human host by crawling in through their open mouth and setting up home in their intestines. From here they send out hundreds of tentacles with which they hook into the host's brain and spinal column in order to take control. Once they have finished with a host, they move on to the next, leaving the first hopelessly insane or, if fortunate, dead.

Ashnon: An extremely rare form of demon that is capable of the ultimate camouflage: the perfect reproduction of any human being. Unlike the Incubi and Succubi, the Ashnon are invisible to other nether-creatures and, unlike the necrotrophs (whom they hate and kill on sight), they cause no damage to the person they are imitating. They are able to charge huge fees to double as heads of state, monarchs, and VIPs in danger of assassination or kidnapping. Unlike the Necrotrophs, the relationship between the host and demon is symbiotic rather than parasitic.

THE DEMON LORDS

Only the most ruthless and powerful demons are able to maintain a position of power within the Netherworld. In a realm driven by hatred, destruction, and treachery, it is impossible to know who is truly on your side and who is merely plotting to usurp you. Thus the most powerful demon lords have always ruled through fear and tyranny, creating armies of nether-creatures to destroy their adversaries at the merest sign of any uprising. But in recent times they have become complacent; too comfortable in their power, too indulgent of their desires, they did not react to the Machiavellian machinations of the vampire Caliban and foolishly allowed him to form a powerful army of his own.

NETHERWORLD FLORA AND FAUNA

Like Earth, the Netherworld is host to a diverse array of animals and plants, and many of these are employed by its inhabitants to bolster their arsenal. The Spiders of Nrgal, Skaleb's Brood, the Hell-Boar that guard the gates to Halzog's Palace—all these are common examples of nether-fauna used by the more powerful nether-creatures to protect property, secrets, and treasures. The flora of the demon realm is no less deadly. Poisonous Hagthorn bushes leave anyone unfortunate enough to be stung by them paralyzed so that the plant can feed on their flesh at its leisure. Bael Ivy has been known to infiltrate the bedrooms of its victims at night to strangle them in their sleep, dragging the bodies to the plant's roots to rot and compost there. Almost all the plants are poisonous and their properties are widely used by practitioners of dark magic.

HUMANS IN THE NETHERWORLD

Some humans immerse themselves so utterly in dark magic that the things that mark them out as human are lost forever. They are driven to cross between the realms and enter the world with no light. Their fate is too horrible to mention here.

Acknowledgments

My thanks to:

My agent, the wonderful Catherine Pellegrino, for seeing something in my work that others could not. Thank you for all the help, guidance, and suggestions (and for making me feel warm and fluffy when I needed it most). And to all the other members of the RCW team for their hard work and dedication.

Rebecca McNally, my brilliant (and immensely busy) editor, who helped me to steer my work in the right direction. Thank you for convincing a potty-mouthed author the error of his ways, for making *Wereling* the very best book that it could be, and for enabling it to make it into the bookshops.

My publisher, Macmillan, and the unknown army of people there who have worked in the background on this book without my being aware of it.

Hope and Kyran, for knowing that when Dad closed the kitchen door in the evening, it meant that it was time to be quiet(ish).

And finally, to my beautiful and long-suffering wife, Zoe, who has put up with my moods and writing-induced despair, and who has kept all of us going during the hardest of times. To her, most of all, my heartfelt thanks. Her love and support mean everything to me.

The Friends who made

WEREling

possible are:

Jean Feiwel, publisher

Liz Szabla, editor-in-chief

Rich Deas, creative director

Elizabeth Fithian, marketing director

Holly West, assistant to the publisher

Dave Barrett, managing editor

Nicole Liebowitz Moulaison, production manager

Jessica Tedder, associate editor

Caroline Sun, publicist

Allison Remcheck, editorial assistant

Ksenia Winnicki, marketing assistant

Kathleen Breitenfeld, designer

Find out more about our authors and
artists and our future publishing at
www.feiwelandfriends.com.